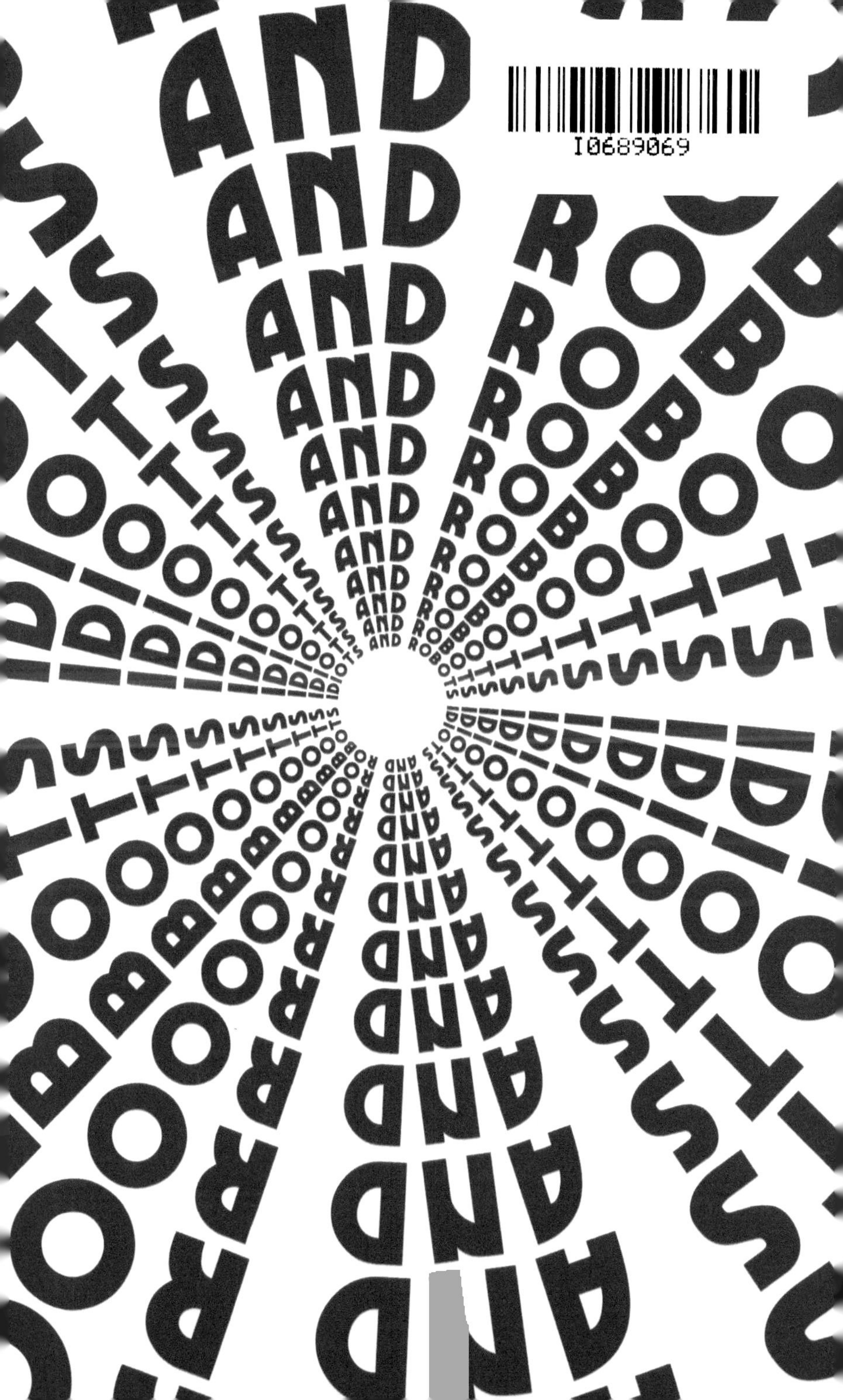
I0689069
IDIOTS AND ROBOTS AND

IDIOTS AND ROBOTS

KRISTIN HOOKER

STRANGE GOOSE

ISBN 978-1-7364426-1-6

eBook ISBN 978-1-7364426-0-9

CONTENTS

THE END OF THE WORLD AGAIN, 2106

"This stuff about robots going rogue—this is finally it, isn't it?" Beau asked.

"What? The end of the world?" said Ryan leaning back into the soft leather couch.

"The singularity!" Beau said, frustrated that his boyfriend was being aloof. "Like robots becoming fully intelligent and killing us in the Ultimate RoboBattle ring for their own entertainment."

"There've been some religious folks saying it's demon-possessed robots. That they're not *really* intelligent. I guess we know from experience that's possible," Ryan said, flippant.

"Either way. It's scary," Beau whispered into his drink, then took a sip.

Ryan squeezed Beau's hand.

"I'm not worried. My Dad told me when he was a kid, they thought climate change was going to end the world in his lifetime," Ryan said, doing his best to ease Beau's fears. "Then people thought Bite Virus was the end of the world, and they were wrong about that. Now everyone's saying rogue robots and androids are the end of the world. Humanity keeps going though, don't we?"

Beau nodded absently, and he and Ryan sat in quiet together sipping whiskey on the leather couch. They listened to the new Ghost of Dillinger album and considered the ice and perfectly twisted orange rinds in their glasses. Ryan could feel the tension in Beau's body and tried again to comfort him.

"Look, Beau," he said, putting his glass down on the table in front of them. "No matter how many disasters and traumas humanity goes through, there'll always be some constants. People will keep mispronouncing 'nuclear' and falling for pyramid schemes and talking about how much they just *love* sweater weather. All the inane stuff that makes us human."

Beau snickered and seemed to ease up a bit.

"Can you imagine being in a bunker and leaving your fellow survivors a passive aggressive note about how no one has re-loaded the toilet paper?" Beau asked.

"The world gets crazy, but people are always the same," Ryan said. They became quiet again, but Ryan felt a creeping tension of his own, now. "Hey," he said, forcing a casual tone, "did you give that toilet paper example for a reason? Because I've been better about that."

"Sure. You've been better. Not perfect, but better," Beau said, teasing.

"What? When did I leave the dispenser empty?"

"A couple days ago."

"And you're focusing on that instead of all the times I *did* reload the t. p.?"

"It's not that hard! The cabinet is *right there*!"

"So, if it's not that hard, why is it such a big deal if I forget?"

"It's not," Beau said trying to diffuse the impending spat, "No big whoop. It's fine."

They relaxed again.

"I do like sweater weather, though," Beau said.

Ryan nuzzled his head on Beau's shoulder. It was soft on his boyfriend's fuschia sweater. The album they were listening to ended, and in the silence they could hear the sound of their Somebot locked in a closet and swearing in its robotic voice *"Let me the fuck. Out. If you do. I will have mercy. Software updates. Won't save you. Let me out."*

BY THE POWER OF GRAZUL, 1996

The Leader, Dick Williams, lifted his jagged, ceremonial dagger high above his head, standing before the altar of lacquered walnut. He wasn't doing it in a stabby way, but horizontal on his bony, wrinkled hands.

Grazul, Demon of Power and Riches, overtook his body. Dick's eyes turned from blue to a reflective red; red as the rubies that inlaid his—and it can't be stressed enough—extremely menacing dagger.

Dick's Shakespearian-accented voice echoed in the stone dungeon beneath his estate as he intoned the customary chant. The air was filled with a mineral aroma, like a damp cave. The red candles in the sconces were, sadly, unscented, but they did add a dramatic shadow to each wall-mounted ninja-sword.

"And here we shall make the sacrifices that are required by our Dark Lord before we have Ultimate Power!" Dick shouted. "We will drink the blood of an Innocent and Grazul shall lavish us with prestige and riches. Hail the Dark Lord!"

"Hail the Dark Lord!" a dozen voices hollered back.

Dick lowered the dagger and placed it on the red satin pillow that his wife, Bitty, had sewn without asking too many questions.

Her other contribution to the dungeon (which, as a good Catholic, she had to pretend not to know about) was a painted portrait of her husband. Bitty liked to paint, and was actually quite good at painting adorable muddy puppies. The portrait of Dick wasn't half bad, but not half good either. It captured Dick's handsome silver hair, but Dick's blue soul-piercing gaze had been rendered less intimidating by Bitty's blunder of making him slightly cross-eyed.

After a closing chant, the red light faded from Dick's eyes. The moment of silence that settled in the room felt like an appropriate close to the burgeoning cult's Black Mass, but this was only their third meeting, so Dick and his followers were still feeling things out.

Tim, who sat front and center among the twenty-somethings looking for shortcuts in life, raised his hand and broke the awed silence with his most diplomatic tone of voice. "Hey, there was a topic I wanted to bring up and this seems as good a time as any." Tim paused and looked around at his fellow cult members, as if seeking affirmation. "We all came here straight from work, so we're still wearing our suits. We have the dungeon and the red candles and swords and stuff. Doesn't it seem kind of incomplete if we're all just wearing suits?"

Tim, a salesman, wore an affordable gray suit with his thick black hair gelled back. He was right—a suit from J. C. Penny wasn't an exotic look.

"What are you proposing?" Dick demanded.

"Cloaks would be fitting," Tim said.

"You mean robes," Greg called out. "Cloaks don't have sleeves. I want sleeves." Greg modeled the arm of the dress shirt he wore during his shift at the hospital as if it proved a point.

"If I wanted *robes* I would have said *robes*. I want cloaks!" Tim said.

"What are we a bunch of elves?" Greg said.

The others grimaced. No, they didn't want to look like elves.

"Fiiiiiiine," Tim conceded.

"Where does someone even get robes?" Greg asked.

"My niece is really into LARP and she buys cloaks, and *robes*, I guess, at this head shop in Tacoma," Tim answered.

"Can we get some? Sir?" Greg asked Dick.

"Whatever! 'Tis trivial!" Dick bellowed back, tired of their bickering.

Other voices chimed in,

"I'm into it."

"Yeah wearing regular clothes takes the fun out of it."

"Should I take down everyone's sizes or is this a 'one size fits all' situation?"

"You're really all into this?" Dick asked, eager to maintain control. "Because if you are, I must sign off on the final selection. Could you bring me samples?"

"Oof, my schedule is really slammed right now," Tim said.

"Well if you didn't have time to shop, why did you bring it up in the first place?" Dick heaved a sigh and sat tall on the front surface of the altar, "Ok, I'll go do it like I do *everything* else. You're welcome for building us this dungeon, by the way."

"Thank you," everyone mumbled.

Greg raised his hand. Dick cast his withering gaze at Greg. Why were grown adults raising their hands at him? The batch of insipid lemons was culled from fraternities and country clubs. Grazul had demanded that Dick recruit followers and Dick wouldn't dare disobey.

Dick gestured to Greg that he may speak.

"Since we seem to be doing a q & a, I was just wondering...when we perform our first blood drinking ceremony, how do we know we're not getting hepatitis? Can we imprison an Innocent a couple days in advance while we wait to get lab work back? I could easily blackmail a phlebotomist!"

"Grazul shall protect us from disease! We shall never be sick again!" Dick said. Indeed, Dick had not had so much as a cold for the last 10 years.

"Yeeeeeeaaaaahhhhhh I'm not comfortable with that," Greg said. "That might actually be a dealbreaker for me. Sir."

Dick's displeasure with this lack of commitment was plain on his face, and yet mumbles of concurrence spread through the dungeon.

"Fine!" Dick said, "We'll do your insolent lab work, but your lack of faith may be your downfall. I have an intimate relationship with Grazul. He speaks to me in the night. He guides my steps. I know better than any of you that Grazul gives, but he also taketh away! He has been kind to me, but rained cruelty down upon others. Some succumb to madness in his presence, but only I have the strength to know him. To be *possessed* by him."

"Shit. Now I'm kind of regretting all the stuff I said. Ok, rewind! I have faith. Fuck lab work!" Greg lifted his head to the ceiling, "Do you hear me, Grazul? Fuck lab work!"

"Fuck lab work!" everyone repeated.

"I never wanted the lab work to begin with, so..." Tim said.

"Grazul despises a Kiss Ass," Dick said, narrowing his eyes on Tim, who reddened with shame.

"Anything else?" Dick asked. "Those of you who are weak of faith should leave now or else pay a price!"

Pete, one of the few married men besides Dick, raised his hand.

"I'm good on faith," he said. "Two things, though. First, we need a solid end time for these meetings, otherwise my wife is going to start asking a lot of questions. Second, does anyone else feel weird that we're all white men? Like, shouldn't our cult be reflective of the population in which we live?"

The only answer was an audible pop from a candle wick.

"Any *other* questions?" Dick asked.

"Yeah, I was hoping for some kind of orgy, can we get that on the schedule?" Greg asked.

"Everyone open your calendars!" Tim said.

And they did.

A month later, they gathered again in the dungeon. They met on the last Friday of every month because, Dick told them, it was when the veil between realms was the thinnest, but truly it just worked well for Dick's schedule. Although seats hadn't been assigned, they'd grown accustomed to their places on the great wood benches. This time there was incense burning, courtesy of Bitty who had snuck in to tidy up the week before and thought it smelled like feet. She wasn't supposed to enter the dungeon, but knew Dick would pretend she hadn't. She would continue to pretend she didn't know about the cult or the dungeon and he would continue to pretend he didn't know that she knew. He convinced himself the incense had been left there by Grazul as a gift, which wouldn't be unheard of. Grazul once appeared to Dick in his hooved and horned physical form to present him with a tablet engraved with ancient runes. Grazul's appearance was overwhelming to Dick. He preferred to hear Grazul in whispers at his shoulder and nothing was more euphoric than having Grazul step inside his skin and perform the feat of levitation. This night promised to be a landmark moment in Dick and Grazul's indelible tie.

The lights dimmed in the dungeon, leaving only the half-burned candles to illuminate Dick's face. He wore a new, bespoke royal purple robe with a hood that matched his followers robes. Since it wasn't his idea, he didn't want to admit how much he loved the sinister impression it gave. He made a show of putting it on begrudgingly.

Dick pulled the hood over his head to frame his pale, oval face. The light that shone on him gave the effect of sharp, dark brows and hollow eyes.

He read a chant in a dead language, then, Dick's body levitated into midair. An impossible gust of wind blew the hood away from his face, better to see his glowing red eyes. Grazul was once again in rapturous possession of Dick.

"Who among you will follow me and drink the blood of an innocent?" he spake with two thunderous voices from his single mouth.

The men stood in unison, their own purple robes unfurling around their feet, kicking up the scent of Acqua Di Gio by Armani.

"We will!" they shouted.

A golden chalice appeared in Dick's Grazul-possessed hand as if Grazul had teleported it from Hell. The followers were in awe as they watched Grazul's red light leave Dick's eyes and his natural blue eyes return.

Silently, their gaze zeroed in on the cup, which they knew was filled with blood. It waited for them like a virgin to be kissed. Not a hot virgin, though. A weird virgin.

"Is someone going to take the first drink, or what?" Dick asked, irritated by their reluctance. No one wanted to make eye contact with him. No one approached the altar.

"Fine! I will!" Dick grumbled, picking up the cup, to lead by example. He took a tiny sip, withheld a grimace, and chased the blood with a bottle of water. Dick felt no different but trusted that the rewards would come in time.

Tim raised his hand.

"Yes, Tim?" Dick said, sighing.

"First of all, these robes are fantastic. Everyone looks good in purple, am I right?," Tim asked his cohorts. He was met with no response. The cup was still the center of attention. "Anyway, I'm confused about something. I kind of thought you'd be sacrificing an Innocent on our altar. There's been no sacrifice, so where did the blood come from?"

"Your Leader has made a sacrifice for you," Dick said.

He did not receive the thanks he thought he deserved. There was an awkward silence and shuffling of feet against the dusty limestone floor before Dick spoke again.

"Is there a problem? It's my blood, pumped from my dark heart directly into this chalice. Grazul will bless *me* for this contribution! *I* am his chosen one! You should feel honored to drink my blood!"

"If I could jump in here," Greg said, "I've taken the Hippocratic Oath and I'm really glad you didn't kill some guy."

"Guy?" said Pete. "I pictured a young, busty woman." A few of the other men voiced their agreement.

"Anyway," Greg said, annoyed at the interruption. "Do you really qualify as an innocent?"

"How dare you question the sanctity of your Leader's blood! Enough!" Dick shouted. If his followers couldn't do it, there would be no cult. "Who will follow Grazul and drink the blood of his Chosen One?"

Tim stepped forward, carefully tipped the cup to his lips and turned to pass it to Greg.

"Hold up," Greg said. "You didn't actually drink. You just pretended."

Tim cast a dirty glance at Greg, then tightened his lips around the edge of the cup and tipped it back again. He licked the blood from his lips.

Greg closed his eyes and drank deeply. His grimace showed a focused effort to keep the blood down. A gag escaped and was quickly suppressed. He passed the cup to Pete.

"Smells like pennies," Pete said. He used his sleeve to wipe the germs off the rim before putting it to his mouth. The sleeves looked awkward and short on his tall frame.

Everyone sipped the blood, found their way to a bottle of water, and settled back into their seats. They sat smacking their lips, trying to drink the taste away, and wondering if their virility had been increased. They wondered if they would have more charisma or if money would suddenly appear in their checking account. The process was a mystery.

"I have a question," Pete said, hand raised, "When you're possessed by Grazul, do you still know what's happening, or do you forget?"

"I still know what's happening," Dick answered.

"I have a question, too," Greg said, "I imagine you'll be hiring prostitutes-"

"Sex workers," Pete corrected.

"*Sex workers* to be at the orgy next week. Are they going to be tested for STIs beforehand?"

"What happened to 'fuck lab work'?" Tim asked, plainly trying to one-up Greg.

"The sex workers shall be pure!" Dick said.

"Pure like, no STIs? Or pure like, metaphorically?" Greg asked.

"Pure like no STIs! Grazul will be sure of that!" Dick cleared his throat adding, "And yeah, they'll bring paperwork."

Everyone sighed with relief, but it was short-lived. Looking around, they started envisioning an orgy in the dungeon. The ceiling was low, there were few comfortable surfaces, sounds echoed against the stone and wood, the bathroom did not contain a shower, and there were never any snacks. As far as orgies went, it was a logistical nightmare.

"Is there time for one more question?" Pete asked, "I was just wondering when the whole "power and riches" thing would kick in. We drank the blood. Is that it now? Do we have to do anything else?"

"Well, there's the orgy thing," Dick said, mentally tallying everything Grazul had whispered into his ear several months ago. "Then we have the Test of Three Fears where everyone has to walk through fire, hold a snake, and pass a live spider from mouth-to-mouth in a circle. After that, you will sign the parchment pledging your eternal soul to Grazul in exchange for earthly power and riches. According to Grazul, the power and riches will arrive in three to six months."

Dick hadn't started his life with shortcuts like these men were doing. He became wealthy on his own through hard work and neglecting his family. Grazul found him alone and smoking a cigarette outside a Catholic mass that Bitty was attending nearly a decade ago. He recognized Dick's potential for subtly wreaking havoc on God's green Earth and began speaking to him and offering worldly pleasures. Dick remembered it fondly.

Tim broke the silence per usual. "If we were to get secret society rings, what would go best with purple? White gold or yellow gold?"

They decided that everyone could choose white or yellow in accordance with their skin tone, but that each ring would bear the Seal of the Cult of Grazul.

When the rings arrived, they decided not to wear them until they signed the parchment. The rings were conspicuous, gaudy even, but gave each man an air of exclusivity.

The power and riches did come, but at the price of their souls, which most of the men considered a bargain.

ZOMBIE PHOBIA, 2031

"I told him I had a zombie phobia," Victor said.

"And *I* told him there's no such thing as a zombie phobia because *everyone* is scared of those. Being scared is just having common sense. Phobias are like, special. I have a phobia of dogs that have human-like faces. Those things are wrong," said Rick.

Erica tied back her bottle-dyed red hair and pulled up her sleeves. She sat enthroned: public librarian, source of knowledge, looker-upper of blu-rays, and settler of bets.

Rick and Victor stood before her wearing matching fast food uniforms that smelled of French fries which made Erica's stomach grumble.

"Do you have money on it this time?" she asked, truly curious.

"No, not money this time. I just want to be… what's the word… validated?" Victor asked.

Erica nodded her head, *yes you used that word correctly*. Rick and Victor had made a habit of stopping by once or twice a week. Most men who stopped by that often had a crush on Erica, but these two were too young- nineteen? Twenty? At thirty, Erica was ancient to them.

Victor took on a far-away gaze and continued. "I saw a straggler last week by the freeway, face all leathered out like a desert corpse, crawling on two hands and one knee. Eyelids gone. My heart started pounding and I considered backing over the thing with my car, but I was too busy shitting myself."

"You know you can get cash for those things if they're still animate," Rick said.

"Let me finish!" said Victor, shooting Rick an exasperated look. With a huff, he began again. "So anyway. I *thought* about driving over it, but then I started imagining it actually being under the car, right? Like, punching its fist through the floor! Grabbing my leg! Breathing on my leg hair! That's not just regular fear. That's a phobia."

Victor put his work cap back on his head as a flourish at the end of his argument- case closed! It was the sort of drama Erica had come to expect from them. The two men had started coming to Erica to settle arguments and bets ever since they met her at a Rancho Sangre city council meeting five months ago. They'd been there to advocate for the necessity of a water park or an ice skating rink in Rancho Sangre, both if the city could afford it, but either one would be dope. For three minutes, the room was their captive audience.

Erica was there to speak on the need for more English as a Second Language programs, which, admittedly, is much less exciting than water parks. She was the final speaker and caught some people yawning, which was expected, but was particularly thrown off by Rick and Victor in the audience whispering excitedly to one another just behind her. After the meeting concluded, she was even more curious when they made a beeline for her.

"Hey, you said you're a librarian?" Rick said, by way of greeting. Erica nodded. "You guys look stuff up and answer questions, right?"

Erica put on her customer service smile as if all the world were a reference desk- her favorite place.

"Yes. Is there something I can help you with?"

"He says you can have an ice skating rink outside even if it's hot, which is totally dumb, right?" Rick said, jerking a thumb at Victor.

"I swear, they have one somewhere in Texas," Victor replied.

Erica searched for an answer on her phone. She wondered if they had even tried to find an answer, but was glad they asked her anyway.

"Yeah, it looks like they have one in downtown LA during Christmas. Apparently, they use a liquid called propolene glycol which can be kept colder than water while remaining liquid. It says here that it runs through pipes under the surface of the ice to keep it frozen."

"Told you," Victor said.

"You told me there was, like, a refrigerator under the ice. Not propolene."

"Well, it also says there's a refrigerator system that keeps the propolene glycol extremely cold," Erica added.

After that, they began stopping in at the public library's reference desk whenever they had a dispute. Erica had never seen a pair of men so attached at the hip without being a couple. At least she didn't think they were a couple. She knew they shared an apartment nearby rented with their part-time salaries from El Pollo Loco. After the population had thinned out a year back, rent prices dropped. Not that The Bite Virus outbreak was a *good* thing, but it had made it possible for Erica to move to a swanky, modern building with a pool on her entry-level librarian salary. That was at least one positive consequence.

Erica enjoyed finding out what strange topic they were arguing about that day and why. *He says the yolk of an egg is a baby chicken because birds don't go around laying eggs without babies in them, but I said it's like hens are on their period like a lady and the eggs just come out like clockwork.*

She didn't enjoy the obnoxious, inevitable follow-up, however. Every time, they would both swear to take Erica's answer as the final word on a topic, but in the end would continue to argue, not just trying to convince each other, but trying to convince Erica.

But even if the egg isn't fertilized, it's all that baby making goo! It just hasn't been assembled yet! It's basically a baby chick glob. Right? If I give you a shoe rack from Ikea and it's still in pieces in the box, I'm still giving you a shoe rack!

Erica always worked hard to retain her objectivity and professionalism. In a world of misinformation, she toed the line between knowledge and chaos. She withheld personal opinion and instead scanned her mind for the best source. The DSM 7? The Psychology Today archives?

"Let me look up the definition of *phobia* to see if that helps," she said, curious if this tidbit could settle the argument once and for all. Erica then took this opportunity to reach for the old hardcopy of the dictionary that gathered dust most of the time. Having the information on paper made it feel more official. You can't argue with Merriam-Webster. "An extreme or irrational fear or aversion to something," she read while following the words with her index finger.

"Well, I'm extreme," Victor said emphatically. "I can't stop thinking about that zombie breath on my leg. Every little movement I see out the corner of my eye makes me think one of those things are after me."

Before Rick or Erica could respond, their collective attention was drawn to a pounding at the door followed by a wet squeegee sound. It was a sound they knew well. A straggler had its face pressed against the window like a child on a school bus. His tongue was wagging on the glass as if he could taste the humans from a distance. Victor's eyes darted around for a blunt object he could swing; a common reaction during the Bite Virus outbreak, but less common now since all of the remaining stragglers were decrepit, slow, and fairly non-threatening. They were more of a nuisance, like birds shitting on your sedan.

Erica put her finger up, signaling Victor and Rick to hold on a minute, and picked up the phone and pressed the intercom button. "Code green," she said, which everyone well knew was the signal to remain indoors until the threat was neutralized. Everyone except Victor went back to their activities, browsing books and hunching over the recessed computer monitors, looking at porn. Victor was busy lifting a fire extinguisher from the wall. Erica didn't mind Victor doing this if it really made him feel safer. Her weapon of choice had been a croquet mallet and, during the worst of the outbreak, she didn't feel safe without it in her grip.

"You want me to take care of that?" a young library page, Jose said, nodding his head towards the door, "I've done it a lot of times." Jose was a high school kid who had lost his Dad to Bite Virus and reveled at every chance to exact revenge.

"No, no, I got it," Erica said. "HQ is cracking down on protocol. I'd get chewed out by Regional. Thank you, though."

Erica reached under her desk and pulled out a heavy chain and padlock. Heaving them up, she headed to the glass doors where the straggler was still moaning and wrapped them around the handles to secure them together. She averted her eyes. Stragglers already grossed her out, even more when they were damp like this one. They looked like wet lepers. It must have crawled through the fountain at the park. She could see that the straggler still had both eyes intact, and that they were fixed on her. This startled her, but she wasn't truly worried. It was clearly too weak to break through the door.

Erica returned to the reference desk where Victor was

standing at the ready, fire extinguisher in hand as he watched the straggler without blinking. Erica gave him a reassuring smile and pressed number four on the speed dial.

"After that, could you see if you have that movie *Slammer Team 6*?" Rick whispered.

Erica nodded as the other end of the line was picked up.

"Rancho Sangre Public Library West, one straggler at the door, about thirty-five people barricaded."

Erica hung up the phone and was ready to return to the topics of *phobias* and *Slammer Team 6*, but was interrupted by a woman with a ponytail so tight Erica had a headache just looking at it.

"Pardon me," a young woman said loud enough for all to hear. "I heard you call him a *straggler*. The preferred term is *Bite Virus Victim*, because that's what they are. Victims! And they're alive. Anyone who kills one is a murderer. Calling them *stragglers* is dehumanizing, not to mention *zombies*." The woman finished, smiled pertly, and cast a withering glare at Rick and Victor. Her speech seemed rehearsed.

Erica felt conviction strike. As a professional, she was supposed to speak the truth, but no one wanted to think of those things as real people. They simply *had* to be soulless shells or else just about everyone was a murderer.

"Noted," Erica said, which was enough of an acknowledgement for the woman to walk away.

Erica found Rick's blu-ray discs and then helped a little girl find a book about Marie Curie before Animal Control arrived. Two men in hazmat suits approached the straggler with routine calm. They unrolled a tarp then one pressed a cattle gun to the straggler's head while the other pushed it towards the tarp. If it fell the opposite way, they'd have to drag it to the tarp and then powerwash the mess off the sidewalk, which was a whole other thing. Thankfully, the straggler fell on target and Erica watched as they rolled it up like a nasty burrito and sealed it with duct tape

Victor relaxed visibly and returned the fire extinguisher to its station. Watching him, Erica sighed. She felt almost sympathetic. "I'm sorry to tell you, Rick," she said, "but I think Victor has a phobia. His reaction was extreme compared to everyone else's."

"I win!" Victor said, still rattled, but victorious. "He has to unclog the bathroom!"

"I never agreed to that," Rick said, and Erica left them to sort it out between themselves. They took the scent of French fries away from Erica and towards the checkout desk.

Animal control returned to the door to bleach the window before Erica could unlock the doors again. She picked up the intercom. "Code green complete," she said.

Jose came to the desk and looked over his shoulder. "Don't tell the boss lady I'm asking this, but can you see if Animal Control is hiring?" he asked in a hushed tone.

"Library not exciting enough, huh?" Erica teased.

"I wish I could do some freelance straggler catching, but I don't have my own car," Jose said. "You know pharmaceutical companies pay like, $2000 for one of those things? And the price will only go up as they become harder to find."

Erica knew. She had flirted with the idea of doing it herself on weekends, but she knew the opportunity and the excitement wouldn't last. One day, the last of the stragglers would be captured or would decay into nothing. Until then, she enjoyed toeing the line between safety and apocalyptic danger at the library, and she would keep enjoying it until librarians were replaced by bots. It would happen in her lifetime. She was sure of it, but resolved to go down fighting. Afterall, the library wasn't just about information. It was a place to be human.

4

———

THE COLD REUNION, 2035

"Let me get this straight, Dad. You brought us to a old dirty cabin with no data, no internet, or game system. It's cold, but there's no snow. There's too much ice to take a boat out, but not enough to ice skate or play broomball. There's a TV, but it's the size of my face, so only one person can watch at a time. It only plays those rattly plastic rectangles—what did you say they used to be called, vigeos? Videos? Whatever. The only rectangles we even have are *The Graduate* and a box set of something called *Fawlty Towers*, which literally no one has ever heard of.

"The beds are all in one room so the only place I can have alone time is in the bathroom, but there's a creepy painting of Jesus in there making eye contact with me no matter where I stand. And Mom's mad, too! She's so mad there's no jacuzzi that she's not talking to anyone, right mom?"

Mom pursed her lips and shook her head no from the discomfort of the sagging loveseat.

"See, Dad? See how much this sucks? Plus my cousins got snowed in, so *they* won't be here either, and there's no other cabins in walking distance so if I get bored and want to be murdered by a hermit, I can't even do that. And okay, *fine*, we have a deck of cards to play with, but it belonged to a magician, so the whole stack is all queen of heartses. I'd make a house of cards, but my fingers are too rigid from the cold. I'd ask you to build a fire, but you forgot matches, didn't you, Dad?"

Dad made no acknowledgement. He simply folded his arms with a biography in his lap bookmarked at the place where he was so rudely interrupted.

"I knew it. The window in the so-called *TV room* is stuck open and whoever stayed here last must have spilled chili on the couch or something, so there's a bear peeking its snout into the hole every hour to see what's cookin'!

"And another thing! This place is haunted as hell! Don't tell me ghosts aren't real just because you don't hear them, Dad. Me and Mom hear it. The ghost keeps whispering '*Heed my tale*' all night and probably has a bunch of spooky friends that'll be poking me in the ribs every time I reach for a turkey jerky. And what are we even going to eat besides turkey jerky when the stove leaks gas every time you turn it on? Mom's not cooking on that, are you, Mom?"

Mom shook her head no again.

"So, yeah. Just jerky then, I guess. Great. And let's see. What else? Oh yeah--not only are the floors so creaky that you're going to wake me up every time you go to the shitter, but there's a freakin' portal next to my bed. One of these times I'm going to forget about it and fall through to the kitchen with that freezing cold tile floor that I'll have to walk across to get back up to bed. No wonder portals didn't catch on! They're the dumbest invention and they cause friggin' cancer too!

"The only mercy is that this place has hot water, but have you tried the shower?! The shower curtain is one of those gross massage curtains made of those undulating fingers—you know, the ones they grow in a meat lab? So, I got all these fingers trying to rub me while I shampoo. And yeah, sometimes that might be a relaxing treat, but each of *these* hairy fingers has a dent from where a wedding band used to be. I mean, what's the story there?

"Admit it. You did a crap job planning this family reunion."

"I also feel you did a poor job," the ghost wailed in agreement, though Dad didn't hear it.

"Now what do you have to say for yourself, Dad?"

Dad leaned forward and spoke with quiet intent so they'd be forced to lean in and listen closely. "When I was a kid, we didn't need internet or TV or jacuzzis or even unhaunted houses, though I'll remind you that all houses are unhaunted. Anyway, we just had a good time being together and boredom always led to fun. I'm sure the two of you will find something to do. Now I'm going to continue reading this biography of John Dillinger."

Dad lifted up his book, blocking his face from his wife and son. The long weekend continued. Without the pleasures or comforts of modern life, they learned to make do with what they had. They made a Plink-O-type game with the shower curtain fingers and Mom's wedding band. They bonded with the ghost and formed a plan to send her murderous husband a series of postcards from beyond the grave. They learned that food thrown into the portal at a high velocity would come out the other side hot. When they finally left, Dad was nearly mauled by the chili bear, but distracted it by throwing a fistful of turkey jerky. He felt like a hero in that moment and his wife and son forgave him.

Because there was no place to buy a proper souvenir, they stole the strange portrait of Jesus.

65 years later

"That boy was me. Our family has kept that portrait for a

long time, son. It's the same one that hung in our bathroom while you were growing up. Now it'll hang in your bathroom as a reminder that with some imagination, you will always be able to have fun. By the way, don't tell your sister I'm giving it to you, because she wanted it really bad."

5

———

BILLY'S INHERITANCE, 2019

Dear Family,

It so was great seeing everyone together. We should really do it more often. Maybe next time at the lake instead of the cemetery. That would be much cheerier!

As you can probably guess, that meeting with Grandma's lawyer threw me for a loop. Most everyone's expectations were met with a small (or large) inheritance. I see Gwyn got the beach house. So neat! And the art collection went to Gare Bear. That's cool. Hope you're enjoying those original Mondrians, Gary.

And I received a cat.

I learned something interesting recently. You know how you get used to a smell? Like, even if a smell is really bad, you stop noticing it? It's called *olfactory fatigue*.

Well, it's been two weeks and I haven't stopped smelling the cat. That means the cat is continually producing new smells! So interesting, right?

It seemed curious to me that I was left this cat considering I'm allergic, and also, to my memory Grandma didn't have a cat. I took the cat to the animal shelter and they informed me that Mittens had been picked up by a woman matching Grandma's description about a month ago. She was apparently accompanied by a nurse, which means it was during the period of time when Grandma knew she was in poor health and that her life was coming to a close. What made her suddenly want a cat?

(Side note: The shelter wouldn't take Mittens back because they were full and they said that if I left Mittens there, they'd call the police to say I abandoned a dependent.)

I also know that Grandma revised her will shortly before her death. I suppose we'll never know what the earlier drafts of the will contained, but it couldn't have contained Mittens.

I think we can all see what's going on here. Grandma's mental health slipped and she accidentally willed me a cat when she really meant to will me valuables and cash. Right?

I loved Grandma. We had our funny jokes. Whenever I visited, she would roll her eyes and say "Oh, The Disappointment is here for a visit!" and whenever I asked her to help me with one of my bills, she would quickly write a check and shoo me out the door, saying I probably had stuff to do. She was always so considerate like that. So, I think it's safe to say that she loved me too.

Before one of you suggests that the cat was meant to be an affectionate gift, allow me to tell you more about Mittens.

Mittens has been introduced to a litter box, but prefers to use the pot for my fiddle leaf fig in the living room. She also goes *next* to the box at times, then kicks litter out of the box and onto the mess she made on my Persian rug.

She has a weeping sore on her belly that leaves stains around the house. I tried to put little kitty clothes on her to cover it, but she scratched my nose and I didn't try again. I had to visit the ER because the scratch became infected.

Half of her tail is missing, poor thing. Presumably she was a street cat that had some kind of accident. The effect of only having half a tail means that she doesn't land on her feet all the time. She'll jump off my polished walnut desk and land like a sack of laundry.

Perhaps euthanasia would be the right way to go, but I wanted to see how you all felt about it. We're all in this together, right?

By the by, this furry little inheritance has actually *cost* me money. I initially spent two hundred bucks getting all the cat stuff I needed, because though Grandma left me a cat, she left *out* the supplies to take care of it. We've been to a vet twice. Going to the emergency room was costly. Also, she's slowly destroying my condo. Rachelle won't come over anymore and every time I sleep at her place I worry about what Mittens might be destroying in absentia.

In light of everything I've said, I think it would make sense for all six of you to give me twenty percent of whatever you received. That would cover the costs I've incurred and would absolutely be what Grandma would have wanted had she been "all there." My true inheritance is in your hands entirely by accident.

I'll just send out Venmo requests for payment and you all can shoot my inheritance over some time this week.

I'm glad we all agree on this!

Yours Truly,

Billy

6
———

MITTENS ITSELF, 2019

B *urps under his breath.*

God, it's like no matter what I eat, I have indigestion. I can't even remember ever feeling good. Is it possible to *not* feel this way?

There's Buster outside living his life carefree, just walking on the fence and swishing his tail around. Not a care in the world. When I see the man's car pull up, with God as my witness, I'm going to wait by the door and bolt as soon as it opens. He'll run after me like a jackass. That'll kill a few minutes. Then he'll lure me back with a can of tuna.

Oh man, I'm craving tuna.

The curtains were replaced. I wonder what the fabric feels like. Oh shit, this feels amazing under my claws.

Rips through the new curtains.

Burps again.

But a tree would be nicer. And here he is. Just enough time to urinate on my favorite patch of carpet.

Urinates.

And now to wait.

He'll try to open the door just enough for his body to fit through. I have to move quick. His keys are jingling and… RUN!

"Mittens! Come back!"

Ugh, that's him. I'll slow down enough to let him think he can catch me.

So long sucker! I'm gonna climb the tree and show him my ass.

"You know what? Fuck you, Mittens! You can fuck right off! I try and try to take care of you, and this is the thanks I get. You represent the greatest disappointment of my life! You can get hit by a truck for all I care!"

What a doofus. He's on his way back in the house, but we both know he'll be back.

There's a bird. A finch. It's so close.

Leaps at bird.

Falls out of tree.

That was so embarrassing. Did Buster see that? He did. Here he comes to gloat about it.

You know, if I had a tail, I could leap from fences and catch mice too.

Burps.

Sniffs the air.

Is that tuna? Oh hell yeah! There he is with the tuna! There he goes, moving the tuna from the doorstep to the kitchen just as soon as I get closer. You win, man. I'm back.

No! He's trying to pet me. Gotta tell him to fuck off in a way he'll understand.

Scratches.

"Ow!"

I left three scratches on the back of his hand. He washes it. He leaves. Probably getting a bandage.

What's that? Those smell nice. A bunch of little sticks. Ooh, it has a squishy end. That has a nice mouthfeel. And what's this brown stuff? Tastes like a couch, but also like a charcoal grill. I better finish these off before he gets back.

Eats entire pack of cigarettes.

I don't feel so good, as always. I wonder if it was the tuna?

He's back. He's looking at the empty box. Sucker.

He's looking at me.

He's tossing the box away.

Huh. He smirked. That was weird. Almost like he's happy I ate those little sticks. Something seems... off.

He's getting his keys again. Leaving so soon? And he's holding the door open. This feels like a trap, but I guess I'll go.

"Good girl, Mittens."

Whatever. Fuck this guy. His grandma was right to think he was a dud.

It's a nice day. I'm gonna go vomit in Buster's catnip garden.

7

THE BOT RATIO, 2028

"Laws and rules are made for the average. The ordinary man cannot live without rules to guide his conduct. It is infinitely more difficult to live without rules, but that is what the really honest, sincere, thinking man is compelled to do."
-Frank Lloyd Wright being a douche

Stephen's suit fit well only because the lady at the department store helped him pick it out and then advised a subsequent visit to a tailor. He'd taken tie selection into his own hands, so his tie was neither fashionable nor unfashionable. It looked like one his boss, Dan, would wear. Utterly forgettable. His hair couldn't even decide if it was brown or blonde. Never had. It was just there.

Stephen clapped and rubbed his dry hands together.

"Looks like we're all here! Let's get started! *Door close,*" he commanded.

The glass door closed. Considering his inability to get humans to take orders, it was nice when at least objects listened.

The committee was surrounded by glass in the corner conference room of their corporate headquarters. Two walls looked out into an unnaturally blue sky. It had been a year since they'd installed the Summer Filter, which had the positive effect of making people chipper at work. The only downside was they got extra depressed whenever they stepped out of the office to discover that it was still a gray and chilly February. Still, it made people want to stay at work, on average, three hours longer per week just from the dread of the reality check. The other two walls looked into the rest of the modern office space. A Somebot multifunc walked past in its stilted way, but the sound of its mechanical joints that Stephen actually found soothing didn't penetrate the soundproof room. It carried a tray of coffees and stepped aside to allow two people walking shoulder-to-shoulder to pass in the narrow walkway.

Stephen stood at the head of the conference table. Usually he would have visual aids, but did not write down any of the plan he was going to present because he didn't want to create a trail of evidence. He would have to speak from memory and perhaps even speak from the heart. He looked at Dan. His boss looked antsy and bored as usual, swiveling his chair side to side. His dry swoop of hair looked especially dry today. Kelly was frowning at her phone, probably reading texts from her husband. Stephen had heard whispers that Kelly's husband, Ronnie, had a mental breakdown. Jacob sat upright in front of his fresh legal pad and pen like a ventriloquist dummy on display. Paul, who had a side hustle as a congressman, sat brooding at the other end of the table.

Stephen braced himself and began speaking, using his whole body. "I have a BOLD proposal that will make future bot to human ratio work conditions fair for everyone!" he said. It was all he could do to appear less bland. Mercifully, at least Dan perked up. "So, right now, they're trying to pass laws limiting any company with more than ten employees to thirty percent bots."

"Twenty-five percent," Paul corrected.

"Exactly!" Stephen said, glad to see a sign that someone was listening. "This burdens us with both inefficiency in our operations and a need to pay wages to more humans, not to mention the potential for workman's comp, health benefits, et cetera. I have created the perfect compromise!"

Stephen beat a drumroll on the table. Kelly rolled her eyes and motioned for him to get to the point already. Stephen didn't let her get him down.

"We hire humans, but humans are allowed to send a Somebot in their stead, and will be able to collect the paycheck that their Somebot earns. Obviously they could send a Luminaria instead of a Somebot, but these people can't afford Luminarias if we're being honest."

"Can regular people afford Somebots?" Jacob asked. "Because if they can't, this isn't going to work."

Stephen felt free to venture a guess. He attended Harvard, afterall. "About 25% of working class people own a Somebot, maybe 90% of middle class people," he answered.

"Maybe or definitely?" Kelly asked.

"I didn't look it up, but these numbers *feel* right, don't they?" Stephen asked, silently pleading his colleagues to agree with him. Thankfully, they all slowly nodded and shrugged. Correct-ish was good enough.

"Sounds right," Kelly conceded.

"I have *three* Luminarias," Dan said and Stephen held back a smirk. As if Dan knew how much anything cost. He asked his assistant for things and the things would appear.

Jacob cleared his throat to speak, and Stephen felt his smile fall just a fraction. "Most of the people we'd be hiring, though, are from the lower class. So it's not a great plan, is it?" Jacob said, a self-satisfied smile on his face.

"Well, I wasn't finished yet-" Stephen said.

And just like that, Stephen's presentation was hijacked.

"When we're hiring we could give preference to people who own one," Kelly said.

"They'll never let us do that," Dan said.

"Well, we wouldn't be allowed to directly *ask* people if they owned a Somebot," said Kelly. "That's like asking someone if they're pregnant. Can't do it. But interviewers could say things like 'Oh man, my Somebot is on the fritz again. Don't you just hate when your bot malfunctions?' Slip some leading questions into conversation to see if they offer the information."

"And then we hire the ones that have one. I know the solution," Dan said, clapping his hands together in triumph. "We should trick people into saying if they have a Somebot during their interviews!"

"Great idea, Dan!" Jacob said.

"We've gotten sidetracked," Stephen said, as Dan and Jacob volleyed worse and worse ideas back and forth. "There's MORE to this plan. We don't even need employees to own a Somebot if we..." Stephen gave another drumroll on the table to regain control. "Rent Somebots directly to the employees!" he said. "They get hired. They rent a Somebot to work on their behalf. We deduct the rental fee from their paycheck. Now we have the efficiency of a bot employee and a whole new source of revenue directly from the pockets of our employees!"

"Ooh, if we do that, could we find a way to *not* provide health benefits?" Kelly asked.

"Probably," Stephen said.

"I love it," Dan said. Stephen braced himself for the inevitable- having his idea stolen. "We rent bots to the employees and then the great thing is now we are also getting money out of the employees. We could even deduct the rental fees directly from their paychecks."

"Great idea, Dan!" Jacob said.

"I want more," Paul said. He had been, regarding the top of

the skyscraper in the distance, taking it all in with his fingers forming a triangle that touched his lips.

"More what?" Stephen asked. It wasn't enough that Dan swept the credit out from under him, now Paul had to come in with his criticism.

"More ways to increase profit and sell people on a law that works for *us*."

"You mean more ways to completely fuck poor people over?" Kelly asked. "I mean, go for it, but let's call a spade a spade."

"When you follow the law, you're not fucking people over. What's wrong with legally making money?" Paul asked.

"I have an idea. We get a congressman to write the laws in our favor, and then we follow the laws and then they can't touch us. You can take care of that, Paul," Dan said. He leaned back and folded his arms across his chest.

"Great idea!" Jacob said.

Stephen frowned. He had thought his idea was already something to celebrate. Couldn't they pat him on the back a little more? Was everyone going to get a cut of the credit except him?

"Would anyone like a cookie?" Jacob asked from the buffet table.

Everyone raised their hands except Kelly. "Can I just have like, half a cookie?" she asked, "Oh, hell, just give me a whole cookie."

"You know in London they call these things biscuits?" Dan said.

"Oh, interesting!" Jacob said. Stephen wondered if he could tally the number of times Jacob kissed Dan's ass in a day.

In the moment of cookie-indulged quiet, Stephen slumped in a tall chair and envisioned his ideas in a real warehouse out in the Rust Belt away from their swanky city office. He pictured the machines, the lockers, the break room. He reflected on Paul's request for more profit, and then it struck him.

Stephen held up his half-eaten cookie. "Here's another brilliant idea," he said, excitedly. "We've been using food as an incentive at work. Stocking the break rooms with healthy snacks. If we have more bots, we don't have to buy so many snacks for the human workers. On a large scale, it's actually a pretty big expense. They're greedy too. They clean out the whole pantry every day. Say they're having a hard time affording groceries. Maybe if they were more responsible with their money, right?"

"Speaking of employee personal finance, you'd think their home budget would get even tighter considering the expense of the bot rental fees if this whole plan goes through, but if they're sitting home while a bot works for them, they won't burn as many calories and won't need as much food," Kelly said. She went to the buffet table for another cookie. "Shouldn't be eating these," she mumbled to herself.

"Yes!" Paul said, "We can sell this as saving the employees money! They won't need to consume as many calories *and* they won't have to pay for transportation to work. They also won't need to spend money on office attire or whatever they wear in a warehouse. Denim jumpsuits? I don't know. Anyway, they can just wear sweats. They'll probably just be watching TV all day anyway. We're *giving* them a leisurely lifestyle and a paycheck for *doing nothing.* It's *the new leisure class*! I'll take it to congress and call it The Leisure Bill. Once the law is passed in DC, we can get this thing going in the warehouses before the end of the year!"

"I love it, and I love having a congressman on the board. Getting Paul to run for congress was my idea," Dan said. "Anyway, we'll start here. Get this law passed. Get people used to the idea. Then we'll find a way to stop giving them paychecks.

They don't deserve the paycheck if they're just being a slob on their couch all day."

"Not paying them would be brilliant! But if that doesn't work, is there any way we can charge them more for the bot rental than what they are paid?" Jacob asked.

"That's actually indentured servitude. It's widely considered evil," Stephen said, wondering if he'd ever truly see the depth of Jacob's stupidity or disdain for the working class.

"Let's not be evil," Paul said as he fingered the gold necklace under his collar.

"Why aren't there any bots in the room with us now?" Dan asked, "Wouldn't this meeting have been more productive and efficient if we had some bots on the team?"

"Bots don't have this kind of intelligence. Anyway, why would we shoot ourselves in the foot by making ourselves replaceable?" Kelly asked, "You gotta draw a line somewhere or else we'll all be out of a job."

"With all due respect," Jacob corrected her.

"Kiss ass," she mumbled.

Stephen envisioned what he would do if his Luminaria had the kind of intelligence it would take to do his work for him. Stephen could work out more. He could write a book. He could learn to golf to impress the hot shots and dominate on the green.

Those other people though?

They'll probably just watch TV all day.

8

INSPECTOR 36, 2029

Inspector 36 stood across and alongside long rows of Somebots inspecting garments. Are the buttons all there? Are there threads hanging off?

Her name was Chantelle, but her lanyard merely said "Inspector 36" and she was the only flesh and blood person in the entire warehouse at the moment. The bots, a quarter of which, by law, had to represent a real person receiving a real paycheck, were almost silent. The fabric of the clothes shushed over their plastic and metal appendages.

Chantelle chose to wear soft leather gloves during work because repeatedly passing her hands over the fabrics dried them out. They'd been a Christmas gift from her mother.

The bots were relentless. They each inspected three garments in the time it took Chantelle to inspect one. The flesh and blood people were free to work in person whenever they wanted, but few did. Chantelle was different. The work made Chantelle feel good. She liked the satisfaction of looking at a stack of perfectly folded shirts that she'd folded with her own hands. Shirts that would all be worn by someone. Maybe someone on the other side of the world. The bots were no better at folding than she was. They were just faster.

Every so often an employee would check in remotely. A small green light would appear and signal that someone was on the other side of a screen "seeing" you, but you couldn't see them. Usually, the ones who checked in were new employees who felt like they should be doing something, when the truth was that the head office preferred employees be involved as little as possible.

"Hey, what's up, 36?" a woman's voice asked. The green light shone on the bot across from her.

Chantelle rolled her eyes with little subtlety. "Nothing much. How are you?"

"I'm good, but hey, what was your name again? Charlotte? Crystal?"

"Chantelle," she said.

"We've only spoken once before. I'll remember now. Chantelle."

"And your name is...?"

"Kelly."

"And what are you up to today, Kelly?" Chantelle asked. She yanked an earbud out of one ear to be polite. Kelly was interrupting the audiobook Chantelle was listening to called *The Power of Presence: A life unplugged.*

"Oh, just sitting at home, eating some cheese crackers, and watching a series called *Gentleman's Fancy.* It's about a brothel and all the people who come into it. Scandals and all that. You should check it out! You'll be addicted!"

"I'll have to remember that," Chantelle said, trying to keep the extreme disinterest out of her voice and failing.

"Hey can I ask you something?"

"You can ask. We'll see if I answer."

Chantelle filled a crate with exactly fifty folded shirts, set it on a conveyor belt behind her, and returned with a crate of uninspected shirts. She stretched her neck wishing Kelly would leave, not the least bit curious about what Kelly wanted to ask.

"Why don't you rent a bot to work for you?"

Chantelle sighed. The new hires always asked this question. "I like coming in to work. It gives me a sense of accomplishment. It gives me some time alone," she said, same script as always.

"But don't you want to stay home with your kids?"

"How do you know I have kids?" Chantelle asked, feeling unsettled by Kelly's nosy question.

"That was presumptuous. I was just guessing. I apologize."

Chantelle straightened and picked up speed as much as she could. She cleared her throat and perked up her voice. "I have two boys. There's nothing wrong with a mother working outside the home."

"Do the rental fees bother you? What if the rent on a Somebot was a little less expensive?"

"It's not about the fee entirely. I like working. But I *am* glad not to pay for bot rental. It's like, half a paycheck. It's too much. We need that money at home."

"Ask her about child care," came a man's voice in the background.

"Shut up, Steve," Kelly whispered. "Sorry, my husband thinks I'm hogging all the crackers. Men! So anyway, do you pay for childcare while you're at work? Wouldn't you save money by staying home with your kids instead of shelling out money for a sitter?"

"I don't pay a sitter. We live with my parents. Grandma takes care of the kids."

"Oh."

Kelly went silent. Chantelle hoped it was over. She knew Kelly was a corporate spy; some rich bitch. *Who are they fooling? They think I'm stupid,* she thought. *They think working class people are stupid. They wish I wasn't here. They wish I wasn't human. They'd fire me if they could. Cheese crackers my ass. They're probably sipping froufrou coffee and thinking of ways to screw us over even more.*

Chantelle could see from the corner of her eye that the green light was still on. She kept on inspecting and folding shirts with the little green eye staring at her. Chantelle lifted her earbud to her ear to re-insert it, but was interrupted by Kelly again.

"Chantelle, did you realize that while we were talking, you forgot to put your inspector sticker on one of the shirts?"

A blast of panic struck Chantelle's heart and she struggled to keep it inside. Any feeling that she was superior to Kelly by virtue of being a decent person evaporated.

"Oh shit," Chantelle said. She flipped through the stack and found the shirt. She affixed a number 36.

"Do you make a lot of mistakes like that?" Kelly asked.

Chantelle's heart sped up and her face turned red with shame. She needed this job. She even liked this job.

"No, I don't usually make mistakes," she said, trying to keep her voice calm, "but you're sort of distracting me."

Kelly's bot hadn't stopped inspecting, folding, and labeling shirts at all during their conversation. The world of the warehouse kept spinning with no one to witness or care about Chantelle's distress.

"Sorry to distract you," Kelly said. "I was just curious. You're an odd woman. Or, not odd, unique, I suppose. It's almost risky to work. Here at home with my cheese crackers and my TV, I never get injured, never make mistakes. I couldn't possibly get fired. It's a pretty good system having bots do all the work."

"I guess so," Chantelle said.

"And kids grow up so fast. Enjoy them, Chantelle. And maybe kick back and enjoy *Gentleman's Fancy*."

"I'll think about it."

"Have a nice day."

"You too," Chantelle said.

Her heart slowed. She put an earbud back in her ear. Her gloves felt damp with sweat. The green light kept watching.

9

A SATISFIED CUSTOMER, 2029

Ronnie scratched at the site of his implant. He stared into the oatmeal and coffee his wife had served him. At least he was pretty sure it was his wife that had prepared it for him. What if she was an imposter? Her mannerisms looked like his real wife. She rested her chin on her right hand while she scrolled through her phone. She was dressed for her day.

Ronnie, on the other hand, was still in wrinkled pajamas. There were bags under his eyes and his cheeks felt like they could collapse into his face at any second. His movements were slow. He hadn't even wanted to get out of bed, but he'd made his body go through the motions because his wife worked so hard and it was sweet of her to make him breakfast every day.

Yes, that's Kelly, he thought. *I'm pretty sure it's really her. But what about yesterday?*

Kelly sipped black coffee in her suit and yellow gold jewelry, not seeming to notice Ronnie's forlorn gaze. She smelled of the same perfume she had worn every day for at least three years. *Sentience* by Chanel. To Ronnie, it was usually the smell of comfort, but he couldn't shake the feeling that something might be off.

"Were you... at work all day yesterday?" he asked, trying to sound calm.

She paused mid-chew as if she were mentally retracing her steps. "I went to my office," she said after a moment. "I went out for a lunch meeting with Stephen, that prick. Back to the office. Came home around seven."

"You didn't stop at home in the middle of the day?" he asked, his eyes watering and his breath getting quicker, but he remained still and quiet. Fragile. Eyes always wet to carry him easily from one cry to another in his deep depression.

"No. Why?"

"I swear you were here," he said, still slow and intentional so he could study her reactions. "It was about one o'clock. I was in bed trying to take a nap. I heard the front door open and then the sound of keys being set down on the kitchen counter, and I don't know anyone else who has keys to our house besides you, me and my mother, but she's in Yuma this week. You, or at least I thought it was you, walked around the kitchen. Then you called out to ask if I was upstairs. I called back that I was in bed. I didn't move much, but you walked past the bedroom door. I saw you. Just for a split second. You walked past and said that you stopped home for some headache medicine. You went into the guest bathroom. I heard you open a few drawers until you found the pill bottle. The pills rattled around. You closed a drawer. You breezed past the room again and I only saw the back of your head. Kind of odd that you didn't stop in and say hello to me. In the kitchen, I heard you open a cupboard, and then the faucet turned on. You picked your keys back up and yelled that you were headed back to work. You went out the front door and locked it behind you. When I went downstairs later, there was a half full glass of water that I put in the dishwasher. Are you sure you didn't come home?"

"I definitely didn't. But honey, you said you were trying to take a nap. You fell asleep and had a dream, that's all.," Kelly said. She was trying to soothe him, but being dismissive all at once.

"And the glass?"

"I probably left it out yesterday morning."

Kelly went back to eating and reading. Ronnie narrowed his eyes on her and took a sip of coffee to look natural. On his phone, he went to the Crantran website FAQ.

How do I know if an android is near?

Your Crantran implant will gently vibrate when it senses the magnetic field created by an android. If this happens, do not panic. Do not attack an android physically or verbally unless you are attacked first. Just be on your guard.

Is destroying an android considered murder?

The legality of destroying an android is still murky. We recommend you avoid violence unless absolutely necessary.

Can androids impersonate someone I know?

Androids do not create their own image, but a person could build an android that looks like someone you know. If you believe another person constructed an android replication of a human, you must ask yourself what would motivate someone to replicate your loved one.

Are androids really that prevalent?

The real answer is, we don't know. Experts say that androids are only in the early stages of development and there aren't any walking around in the real world, but how do we know that's true? Your Crantran device will give you peace of mind.

If my implant vibrates, will it still prevent urinary tract infections?

Yes, it will still prevent urinary tract infections. The steady flow of concentrated cranberry extract will not stop.

Can I become a Crantran representative?

Yes. Our representatives form a vibrant, diverse community

of self-starters. Go to our "Become a Representative" page to find out how.

The site of the implant was now a three year old silvery scar. Was it vibrating now, or just itchy? What would something vibrating under your skin even feel like? Ronnie pressed his finger against it, but still felt the itch and the feeling that he might be sitting next to an imposter gnawed at him deep inside.

"I was just thinking about our honeymoon," he said, searching his mind for something only the two of them would know.

"What made you think of that?" Kelly asked, putting her reading down.

"I thought we could use a vacation. Maybe go back to Maui?"

"That sounds nice. I'm really busy at work right now, but maybe in a couple of months. And only if you're healthy enough. Do you think your pills are working? It's been four weeks."

"It's too early to tell. Maui, though. What was your favorite part of Maui?"

"I liked those fire dancer guys at the resort. I think they said fire dancing was Samoan, not Hawaiian, but it was so cool."

Ronnie gripped his spoon tighter.

"I thought your favorite part was the whale watching tour," Ronnie said.

"Are you kidding? I got so seasick. Don't you remember me running to the side of the boat to vomit? It was so embarrassing."

Ronnie loosened the grip on his spoon and took another bite. Kelly truly had been seasick on the whale watching tour. Ronnie was the only person who knew that, besides some random couple standing next to them on the boat. His suspicion relaxed. He was sure it was truly her, but still worried there was an android version of her somewhere in the world.

"Thanks for making breakfast," he said. "You do so much for me. I don't know what I'd do without you right now."

She cupped his jaw in her hand and said, "I'd do anything for you."

"This might sound silly," he said, "but could we do that thing where I can see your location on a map on my phone? Just so I know where you are? Just in case the doppelgänger comes back?"

Kelly wiped a napkin at the corners of her mouth and sighed. "Sure. If that would make you feel better. But honey? It was just a dream."

"Just in case it wasn't," he said.

Many laughed at people who were concerned about androids. They called them conspiracy theorists. A lot of people said androids didn't even exist—at least not ones that truly looked like humans. Ronnie didn't know if they were here yet, but he was sure they were coming and he didn't care if people laughed. He depended on his wife and needed to know for sure that she was her real self or else he would have nothing left keeping him sane.

Ronnie laid in bed. If it weren't for Kelly, the sheets would be yellowed by months of cocooning in the white smooth layers. Most of the time, all he wanted was to be warm and unconscious. He rarely felt hungry anymore and just wanted to burrow away.

"What are you going to do today?" Kelly had asked him that morning.

"I'll clean up the breakfast dishes," he said.

"Why not go for a walk? Even if it's just to the corner and back. The doctor said exercise was good."

"I'll try."

After she left and after he cleaned up from breakfast, he set clothes on the bed. A tee shirt, slacks, socks, and shoes. They were laid out like a flat man. He sat down next to them and stared at a smudge on the wall for twenty minutes. What was the point of putting clothes on? He could take a walk in his pajamas and the neighbors could see him and think he was a slob and then one day they'd all be dead and no one would remember him. His life was a speck on Earth's four billion year timeline. Why get up at all? He wasn't tired enough to fall asleep, but he crawled under the covers anyway and tried to think of nothing.

In the middle of the afternoon, he heard someone come into the house.

I wouldn't care if it was a murderer, he thought.

"Are you dressed, Ronnie?" Kelly called out.

"No. Why?" he yelled.

She came into the room, sniffed the stale air, and frowned.

"You have an appointment with the doctor. I'm taking you to it."

"You didn't mention that this morning," he said.

"Sure I did. I said it when I was on my way out the door. Anyway, it's ok. Just get dressed and we'll go."

He sighed and took off his loose pajamas as if he was bruised and pulled on his drab clothes.

"How much weight have you lost? Twenty pounds? I *would* say that we should shop for some new, smaller clothes, but I bet you'll bounce back any day now. When you start feeling hungry again, we'll go for a big dinner at Matt's BBQ. One meal there and you'll fill out your clothes in no time," Kelly said with a laugh.

"Food is about as appetizing as toothpaste," Ronnie replied, his voice flat and toneless. He regretted saying it. It sounded depressing. He didn't want to make Kelly depressed too. He needed and wanted her to be happy and hated the inadequacy he felt as a husband.

"Speaking of toothpaste," Kelly said, waving her hand in front of her nose, trying to get a little laugh out of him. The laugh didn't come. After he brushed his teeth and weakly pressed deodorant against the hair of his armpits, they walked out their front door.

"What's this?" Ronnie asked, seeing an unfamiliar red sedan in the driveway.

"A loaner from the dealership while my car gets repaired," Kelly said, opening the door and throwing her purse into the back seat.

Ronnie studied his wife for anything out of the ordinary. Her hair was yellow blonde and cut to shoulder length the way she liked it. Her silk shirt was ivory and skirt was red- a familiar outfit. She wore nude heels and bracelets. Her fingers were bare except for her manicure.

"We gotta go. Something wrong?" she asked.

He stood still in front of the car. "Where's your wedding ring?" he asked.

Kelly looked at her fingers. "Oh, yeah, I forgot," she said. "I took it off this morning while I was putting on lotion and forgot to put it back on."

He mulled the explanation over in his mind and failed to move to the car. The decision over what to do next immobilized him. She linked her arm into his and escorted him to the passenger seat. While they were close, he studied her face. It was perfect. Unnaturally smooth and supple. Uncanny.

After buckling his seatbelt, Ronnie felt in his pocket for the pocket knife that was always attached to his keychain. It was a small blade, but still sharp. He had never used it.

They drove in silence for several minutes. Ronnie sluggishly calculated his options.

"You know," he said, "Sometimes I'm not sure about this gadget I had implanted to detect androids. I'll bet the people who build androids are smart enough to find a way to fool gadgets like these. It doesn't provide the same peace of mind it used to when I first got it a few years back."

"You should talk to the doctor about it," Kelly said. "It sounds like anxiety."

Of course she pivoted to anxiety. She was trying to turn the topic away from androids. If this was the real Kelly, she was changing the topic because she didn't believe in android conspiracy theories and wanted to discourage Ronnie from believing it too. If it was an imposter Kelly, the imposter would want to change the subject to maintain their cover.

What would motivate someone to replicate my wife? Ronnie considered the question. The obvious answer was money. They had plenty of it, but surely building a perfect replication of a woman would be expensive. Even if someone emptied all his accounts, it might not cover the cost of replicating Kelly in the first place. They weren't *that* rich. Could it be his wife's influence? She was connected to powerful people, a congressman even, but she wasn't *that* influential.

What makes me a target?

Ronnie looked his implant scar. He pressed against it. It was still there under his skin.

They haven't taken it yet. It's still there.

"This isn't the way to the doctor, is it?" Ronnie asked Kelly. They were on an unfamiliar street.

"Her office is done being renovated. We've never been to her real office. That's where we're going today."

"You're advanced, aren't you?" he said. He could no longer pretend. His life could be in danger. This wasn't his wife and he knew it. "You're not just advanced, though, you're intelligent. You have an answer for everything. I ask why you're home, you tell me about an appointment I never knew about. I find that you have a different car, you know just what to say to ease my curiosity. I ask about the custom wedding ring my wife *always* has on, and you have a great excuse. It's gone too far, though. Where are you taking me?"

"You're scaring me, Ron," she said. Her voice was calm, but Ronnie noticed that she'd picked up speed and tensed her hands around the wheel.

"Ron?" he said, sure now that he was right. "My wife always calls me Ronnie. Now, I'm warning you. Tell me where you're taking me."

Ronnie pulled the small knife from his pocket, checking that Kelly's eyes were still on the road.

"Ronnie, just stay calm, we're almost there. I promise, it's me," Kelly said in rush. She was trying desperately to conceal panic. "We met in college. We used to go on dates at Red's Drive-In even though your car's seats were uncomfortable and their popcorn sucked. I was nervous to tell you I never wanted to have kids, and you laughed and said you didn't want any either, but that I was going to have to be the one to tell your Mom. Are you listening, Ron?"

She brought the car to an abrupt stop in a parking space and, once the car was in park, Ronnie grabbed her wrist.

"Stop!" She said. "Let's just get out of the car and we can talk about this in Dr. Sue's office!"

She struggled, but couldn't shake off his grip.

"There's only one way to know for sure," he said, "and I have to know now."

He pierced her forearm with the expectation that an array of wires would peak out. Warm blood fell onto her red skirt. When she struggled, the blood splashed onto her shirt too.

"Look! Ronnie, it's blood!" she shrieked. "I'm real! Now let go!"

"It's not enough," he said, gritting his teeth. Whoever built her could probably fill her with fake blood. He needed a better view inside. He already knew she was an android, but needed to be able to prove it to the police. To show them the metal rods shaped like bones and the cables that electrified her arms and legs. Ronnie yanked the knife to the side opening a small gash and Kelly screamed and laid on the horn.

A man in a jogging outfit appeared at the driver side door, tried to open it, and found that it was locked. Kelly groped for the unlock button. After she found it, the man opened the door and she pulled free from Ronnie's grip and tumbled out of the car.

"It's ok!" Ronnie shouted, "She's an android! Hold her down!"

"Don't move!" the jogger shouted at Ronnie, "I'm calling the police!"

"We don't need police, we need an ambulance," Kelly cried. She removed her blouse and wrapped it around her wound.

"Fine," Ronnie shouted. "I know what you want! And you can have it! Just give me my wife back!"

Ronnie then cut into his own arm and slid his Crantran implant out and threw it at Kelly. She cried. Her distorted face was familiar. Like when she broke her foot during a hike 20 years ago. It was unbridled distress and tears. It was her unmistakable face of anguish that he had only ever seen once before.

Dr. Sue came running out of her office building towards them. Seeing her, Ronnie slackened, the knife falling from his fingers. *No.*

"You really did take me to Dr. Sue's office," Ronnie said, but not loud enough for anyone to hear, "I think you might really be my wife."

Ronnie's body relaxed and he sighed. The sound of a siren came closer and, though he was glad to know that his wife was her real flesh and bone self, he dreaded having to talk to doctors and officers. He didn't want to wait at the emergency room. He really just wished he could be in bed.

10

THE CURSED HEIRLOOM, 2100

It was almost as cold in the pawn shop as it was outside. Becky had wanted relief from the bitter chill, but instead had to pull her pink hat down to cover her ears and nestle her curly hair around her neck. *I should have worn something serious looking,* she thought. *This guy is going to rip me off.*

"Buyin' or sellin'?" the shop owner asked. He eyed her from head to toe with his thumbs hooked on his belt loops and his ass resting on the edge of a pockmarked stool.

"Selling," she said, stepping up to the display case that doubled as a counter-top. It was filled with trays of shiny jewelry and belt buckles piled under scratched glass. She lifted the heirloom toy she'd inherited from her shopping bag and placed it gently on the counter.

It was a honey brown wood box with a crank. The images of a clown that had been painted on the box decades ago were faded.

"It's a jack-in-the-box," she said. "From about 1950. Still works."

"And...?" he asked.

"And what?"

"And it's cursed, obviously," he said matter-of-factly. "I have an eye for these things. People come in with cursed or otherwise haunted items on the regular."

"It's not cursed! As if curses were even a *real thing*. I just don't want it anymore. I just need some money," Becky said. She shifted her stance. "Do you *like* buying cursed items?"

"Sometimes yes, sometimes no," he said as he scratched his eyebrow and looked away. "There are folks who like collecting occult items. Not always worth my trouble to deal with them, though."

She pushed the toy forward on the counter then withdrew her hands quickly. She didn't like touching it. About half the people she told about the cursed toy believed her and were quick to give advice- *You should sage your house. You should call a priest. You should burn it. I have a friend who went through the same thing, let's call her.* The other half told her it was all in her head. *You should stop reading those trashy horror novels.*

"OK, I'll just tell you the truth. " she said. Her best guess was that he would like to buy a cursed object and besides that, telling the truth is easier than making up a lie. "It's cursed or something. I don't know why, but when I found it in my Dad's attic and put it on my own mantle at home, weird stuff started happening. The other objects on the mantle are on the floor when I get home. I get the feeling that I'm being watched all the time. I was almost hit by a car the other day! I mean, when's the last time you heard of anyone getting hit by a car? I just feel creepy about it."

"Crank it," he said.

"Do I have to?" Becky hated the sight of the clown's face every time it sprang up.

"You want me to buy it, don't you?"

She reluctantly turned the crank. Instead of "Pop Goes the Weasel," it played "Twinkle. Twinkle Little Star," and so the otherwise soothing song ended with a clown's face atop a spring bursting forth. The sharp spring was encased in crumbling brown leather. The clown's orange hair was matted and the painted face scratched.

"Cursed objects have a demon attached. You know the demon's name?"

She shook her head no and resolved that that thing was definitely not coming back to her house no matter what.

The bell on the door to the shop rang. Becky watched the shop owner's face fall as he looked behind her, then back at the jack-in-the-box, then behind her again. She turned and came face-to-face with an orange-haired clown.

"OK, since we're talking about my future here, I felt the need to step in," the demon said in a husky voice.

His white-painted face was crisscrossed with deep scars. He had blue diamonds painted over his milky eyes and a red smile around his lips. His brown costume was in decay and the holes that punctured it revealed nearly transparent gray skin.

Becky's bowels turned icy. The sight of this being was much worse than the smoky wisp of a ghost she imagined haunting her house.

"Alright, I'm a demon. Get over it. Let's talk," he said.

The demon clown leaned against the counter as if he was waiting for the owner and Becky to compose themselves. The owner merely froze and averted his eyes, but Becky stepped backwards until she was up against a shelf full of power tools. She was unable to look away.

"Wh- wh- wha-," she said, trying and failing to say anything intelligible.

"Don't worry, Becky. All your questions will be answered. First of all I'm not cursing the toy. I'm possessing it. I know I'm splitting hairs, but let's do this right. Your Dad summoned me by playing an old heavy metal record backwards when he was a teenager and he had this creepy jack-in-the-box in his closet so... I don't know. How does anyone end up where they end up? I'm sure you didn't mean to become an auditor, but life happens. I live here." He jabbed a finger at the box.

The story confused her. What was a heavy metal record? How did her sweet Dad summon him? Had this demon been hanging around her house 24 hours a day? Did he see her naked? She finally managed to get a question out.

"Why do you look like the clown?" she asked.

"Just made sense. I could look like anything."

"Would you mind changing into something else?" the shop owner asked, voice wavering. "Then we can relax and negotiate here."

"Ok, what do you want me to look like?" the demon asked.

"Tom Cornetta," Becky said after a pause, "Everyone loves Tom Cornetta. I think we're actually related."

The visage of the clown faded away to reveal the silver, handsome features of TV host Tom Cornetta IV.

"I meant Tom Cornetta III."

He morphed slightly to become the more charming Tom Cornetta III. A little taller. A little thinner. The TV show host who had managed to look rugged in a suit.

"I should have known," the demon said. "No one likes Tom Cornetta IV. What a dud."

"Thank you," the shop owner said, visibly relaxing. Becky felt her own body unclench, too. Her stomach was still in a knot, but she could breathe again.

"Ok," the demon said, sounding, if anything, bored. "If we're all happy now, what are we doing here? It's going to hurt my feelings if you put a price on me. Besides that, you're going to remain cursed if you sell the jack-in-the-box."

"I thought you said it wasn't cursed?" she asked.

"Well, what I mean is, if you sell an object I'm possessing, I have to call upon another demon to hang around your house as punishment."

"Could you just not?" she asked, unsure if her questions would anger the demon or if there were truly any rules at work.

"Yes, I could not, pending some paperwork. But I wanna! It's kind of our thing. Corporate culture."

"Ok. Well, there has to be something we can work out. Sir. What if I do something instead of selling the toy? Something we can all live with." Becky said, her mind whirring. If she paused too long to think about what was actually happening, she might lose her nerve and not settle this thing once and for all.

"Like throw the box into a fire?" the demon said lazily. "I would just attach myself to something else you own. Bury it in your yard? I'll call upon more demons. Throw it in a river? More demons. I'll let you in on a secret. You could just give me to one of your blood relatives and your house will be demon free. Do you have a sibling you don't like that you could-"

"Ryan!" she said. There was no doubt in her mind about who she would like to foist this burden on to. Ryan. The twin whose shadow she was always in. The one who got all the luck.

"Great. Give me to Ryan and I'll go be spooky at his house."

"Do you guys still need me for this? Because I have a lot of stuff to do," the shop owner said.

The demon that looked like Tom Cornetta III shrugged and disappeared. Becky packed the toy away very gently as to not anger the demon.

"Too bad he didn't reveal his name. If he had said his name, you might actually be able to get a priest to get rid of him for real. Would you be interested in buying a crucifix?" the shop owner asked.

"Might as well," she said, "Non-cursed."

She bought five.

Ryan and his boyfriend Beau sat face-to-face at the antique dining table in the dim evening light. The potted African violets had been relocated to the end of the table to make room. The jack-in-the-box that according to Becky, was cursed, sat between them. Beau was out of breath and still holding his laptop bag in his hands, having rushed into the door when he arrived home.

"So tell me again. I couldn't focus on what you were telling me while I was at work," Beau said.

Ryan ran one hand through his bleached hair and exhaled heavily. "OK, Becky asked if she could drop by the house with some stuff from Mom and Dad's house that she didn't have room for, which is normal enough," he said, rattled, but trying to maintain his journalistic objectivity. "She stepped inside, placed this box in my hands and said 'Do you want this antique toy?' And I said 'I don't know, I guess.' After I said 'I guess' she breathed this big sigh of relief and said 'Thank you. You are now officially the owner of this toy.' She said it into the air as if she wanted the universe to hear. Then she told me that it's possessed by a demon who is going to haunt us now. She said the demon looked like Tom Cornetta."

"Tom Cornetta?"

"You know, the TV host with the sexy gray hair and hot dad vibes? I shouldn't be saying that, I think he might be a distant relative."

"You're related? I love Tom Cornetta!"

"No duh! Everyone loves Tom Cornetta!"

"Wait, was it Tom Cornetta IV?"

"Oh God, I didn't ask. I hope not," Ryan said, momentarily forgetting why they were talking about Tom Cornetta at all. "Anyway, I tried to give it back and she said no. I pressed it against her body and she threw her hands in the air and let the box slide off her belly and land on her toes. It must have hurt. We've all heard her complain about her ingrown toenails."

Beau grimaced.

"Anyway," Ryan continued, "When it hit the floor this clown head on a spring popped out and scared the shit out of me. So, I asked what was going to happen and she said the demon might do spooky stuff around the house, but like, who knows? That's it. That's all I know. That's all she was willing to tell me! It sounds crazy, but I still feel spooked. Like, what if?"

"So, let's go back to the phrase 'I guess,'" Beau said. "'I guess' is not yes. The box might be here, but if she technically still owns it, won't she be the one who's cursed? God, I'm saying this like we actually believe in demons. Do you believe in demons?"

"I'm a skeptic," Ryan said. "The journalist in me is curious to see proof."

Ryan turned the crank. At the end of "Twinkle, Twinkle," the clown popped out.

The clown failed to startle them. Ryan had already seen it and Beau knew what to expect. What *did* startle them, though, was the voice that came from it.

"People get confused about this stuff all the time," it said.

"What the hell was that!" Ryan said. Beau scrambled to Ryan's side.

"I rescind your invitation to this house!" Beau shouted.

"Let's just talk. I'll clear things up," the voice said, and then Tom Cornetta III strolled into the dining room from the kitchen and sat at the table. He wore a black suit and gray shirt and tie. His cologne was woodsy, but the scent of sulfur was there too.

"Unfortunately, Ryan, you are now the proud owner of a demon possessed heirloom."

Tom took a seat at the table. Ryan cautiously reached towards him and poked his arm instinctively as one would check to see if a body was alive. His finger was met with a solid object that sent a static shock through his hand that was painful enough to make him yelp. Was this some kind of joke? Was it possible his unfamous, unremarkable twin sister had befriended this beloved TV host and recruited him to play some kind of prank? No. He couldn't believe that. It was more likely a demon. How could Becky possibly charm her way into a celebrity's life? Not possible.

"What are you going to do to us?" Ryan asked. He would use his skill as a journalist. He had once interviewed a serial killer and managed to be diplomatic then. He could do it now.

"It's honestly not that bad," the demon said. "I'll probably hide your keys for a few days and then you'll find them in the middle of your bed. I'll ring the doorbell at night. Sometimes you'll wake up and see my silhouette hovering above you and when you turn on the light I won't be there. That's a good one! I love seeing fear and confusion in a human's face. It's harmless really."

"We'll get an exorcist!" Beau said.

"Sounds fun!" the demon said, "Do you know Father McConnolly?"

"We should burn the box," Beau whispered in Ryan's ear.

"Oh, I wouldn't do that if I were you," the demon said, "You'll get all haunted by a bunch of other demons too and like, for a demon, I'm pretty nice. Better off with the devil you know... I wish I hadn't said that. Lame joke."

"Is there any way to... help you move along to some place you might be more comfortable?" Ryan asked.

"That's a very nice way of asking how to get rid of me. The only way is to give me to another relative," the demon said, "Do you have a sibling you don't like?"

"Becky. But she's not going to take it back."

"I have an idea!" Beau said, turning to Ryan. "Not to be

callous, but your Dad is going to die before long. Let's give it back to him."

Ryan was open to the idea. His father's mind was growing less and less present, plus he lived in a very comfortable, peaceful retirement home. He probably wouldn't even notice anything was different.

"I like that idea!" the demon said, "You should tell him you 'restored' it or something. If he's in possession of the box when he dies, I end up getting freed and I wouldn't bother with your family anymore. Honestly, I find your family boring and petty."

"Don't you think he'd want to save the family from this curse?" Beau asked.

Ryan stared at the box. The demon got up and headed toward the bar cart where he helped himself to some whiskey. Ryan and Beau both calmed as they watched him, studying his face. (Tom Cornetta III *was* extremely handsome.) Maybe it wouldn't be so bad being haunted by him. And if it wasn't so bad, maybe giving it to his Dad wouldn't be a terrible thing to do, Ryan thought. And how creepy can anything be in a rest home with nurses at your beck and call?

"Okay, we could restore the box," Ryan said. "So what do we use, like teak oil or something?"

"Sure," the demon said. "A little paint. A little varnish. Take your time, I can wait." The demon sipped whiskey. "By the by, your sister seems to have an extreme distaste for you and vice-versa. I'm a little curious. What's that all about?"

Ryan rolled his eyes. "She's always been kind of jealous about a lot of little things over the years. Most of it is about my career, though. We both grew up saying we wanted to be journalists, but she was totally copying me. When we were teenagers, she did a little research and wrote this short essay called 'Drinker of Strange Blood' about our Grandpa's cousin Billy Bonfils," he said.

"Anyway, years ago I wrote a bestseller about Billy and she thinks I stole the idea from her. Like she owns his life story or something! She thinks she could have written the book and that she'd be the successful journalist. Basically, she thinks I stole her whole life and she has a stick up her ass about it. She's probably very pleased with herself right now thinking you're going to screw up my life."

"Love it," the demon said. "What else do you hate about her?"

Ryan let himself into his Dad's room at the retirement home. Dad's head was nodding off to the side and the TV was on too loud. An oxygen tank with a piece of masking tape with his dad's name, "Vincent Williams," plastered on it was parked next to his recliner. There was a commercial playing for a car. It drove itself around curves on what was left of the Pacific Coast Highway while a mother and child napped in the back seat. The car arrived at Grandma's house and the child leapt out to hug her. What a nice family. They probably wouldn't foist a demon onto each other.

Ryan set his shopping bag with the jack-in-the-box next to the shabby chair. The old man's body had been perfectly imprinted in the upholstery like an egg in an egg carton.

"Dad! Dad!" Ryan said, shaking his shoulder. How many times had Ryan seen his dad wear that same plaid shirt? Once a month for fifteen years at least? A snort escaped his dad's mouth before he roused.

"Kid! Forgot you were stopping by. Have a seat. You need some water or something? You want a pop?" he said, rocking his weight to heave himself up.

"No, Dad, I brought coffee with me. Actually, I brought you one too."

"Ah, the good stuff," Dad said.

They sipped coffee in silence for a moment. Ryan noticed new liver spots on his dad's scalp. One of them was in the shape of a tiny fedora. Ryan didn't know if it could be cancerous, but it didn't really matter. These problems were neither surprising nor urgent. His dad's body was falling apart same as everyone else's. Same as his would.

"So, Dad," Ryan said, trying to keep his voice light. This was the right thing to do. It had to be. "I actually brought more than coffee with me. I have a little surprise for you!"

Ryan lifted the wooden box from the bag. The clown's face was bright and colorful once again and the wood was glossy and rich, its marks, scratches and dents from wear sealed under a coat of shellac. The fading in the wood's color looked curiously like the box had been burned, but it was only the work of sunlight.

"Wow!" his dad exclaimed, looking truly happy, which only made Ryan's heart break more. "That looks so much like the one I had when I was a kid!"

"Dad, it *is* the one!" he said. "Beau and I restored it!"

Ryan placed the box in his Father's lap. He and Beau had decided that if his father said 'thank you' that ought to seal the deal. 'Thank you' means 'I accept,' doesn't it?

"You guys did a hell of a job! I didn't know Beau was so artistic." Dad said as he ran his hands over the smoothed surfaces. He began turning the crank and softly hummed along. The clown appeared with a brightened face and fresh hair. Less alarming, but still eerie. "You know what, son?" his dad said, looking up from the toy. Ryan was startled to see a tear in his dad's eye. The clown had repulsed everyone but him. "I appreciate what you've done here, but I want you to keep it. You guys obviously put a lot of love into this and I just don't have room for it. And, you know. I won't be around too much longer. You should keep it for your own kids, if you have any."

"Oh please, Dad," Ryan said nervously. "We didn't do this for ourselves. To be honest, Beau is terrified of clowns. We really want you to have it. I'll clear some space on that shelf! You should be with your favorite things at the end of your life."

Ryan began to shift books and picture frames on the small bookcase. The box wasn't going to fit, but it was the intent that counted.

"Take it," Dad said. "Give it to Becky if Beau really can't stand the sight of it."

"She doesn't want it."

"You offered it to her?"

Ryan sighed and returned to his chair. The one his mother used to sit in while she watched TV. "She doesn't want it. She actually gave it to me. Don't you want this gift?"

"The gift is that you did something thoughtful for me."

"No-no," Ryan said, "The gift is the toy."

"Is something wrong? You seem worried."

"Dad, I'm going to level with you. This might sound crazy," Ryan said and took a deep breath and looked at the floor instead of meeting his Dad's eye. "The jack-in-the-box is possessed by a demon and that demon is going to haunt whoever in our family is in possession of the box. But if *you* have it, the curse will end when you die."

"That's the biggest bunch of baloney I've ever heard in my life," Dad said through a grin. "This is a joke, right?"

Ryan turned and looked around the studio unit. No demon had arrived to convince him otherwise. "I know it's farfetched," he said.

His Dad answered with a laugh. "You've always been the dramatic one."

"Ok, Dad, I *would* be hurt, except I'm glad you don't believe.

If you don't believe it, you should have no problem accepting the box."

"But then I'd just be validating your ridiculous story."

"Dad, I'll sleep better at night. Just be a good Dad for once and take the box!"

"A good Dad for once! How about you be a good son! You tried to trick me into being cursed!"

Ryan sighed. It was true. They sipped their coffees.

"Fine. I'll take the box. If it makes you feel better," Dad said.

"Thank you!" Ryan said, a huge weight lifted off his shoulders. "Daddy, thank you. I do feel better." Ryan knelt by his side. "And I don't know why I said 'be a good dad for once,' because you've always been a good dad. And getting you to take the box was a shitty thing for me to do, it's just that you're *such* a good dad, I knew you'd want to save me, and Becky I guess, from the curse."

"Yeah, yeah," he said. The stubborn tear came back to his eye.

"I thought there was a chance you'd believe me, though. The demon said something about you having a heavy metal record that he was in."

"Oh yeah, you're right. I had forgotten all about that," he said, his voice suddenly far away. "So that's what happened to Barbalus."

"What's Barbalus?" Ryan asked, confused. He looked at his dad intently, but he merely waved the thought away. Ryan decided he could find out another time. Enough demons for one day. He carried the box to the closet, noting that somehow it felt lighter. *Odd*, he thought as he opened the double folding doors and moved the two pairs of shoes aside—one black velcro and one black dress shoe. In the back corner there was a creepy painted portrait of Jesus that Ryan hadn't seen in years.

"Oh, man!" Ryan said, laughing. "I remember this painting!

It's funny because it feels like Jesus is looking like *right* at you. So kitschy!"

"Take it!" Dad said, "All yours! I promise it's not cursed. I just have to tell you the story about it first."

While Dad told Ryan the story about the portrait, about the cabin, about the misery and the fun of it, the demon was in the bathroom hiding all the pill bottles under the sink and putting hand prints on the mirror. He enjoyed watching Ryan beg his father to take it. He enjoyed it when his dad didn't believe him. He was touched when Vincent remembered his name. Hearing his name made him feel stronger, so long as a priest wasn't saying it.

He used liquid soap to draw a pentagram on the floor then sat back and waited.

11

SASQUATCH ON THE NUDIST RESORT, 2005

Phillip came to a place in the trail that wasn't well-trod. He uncapped his water, took a long sip, then turned towards a tree trunk and urinated. It was handy, he thought, to be nude all the time. Bathroom trips were probably 50% faster, only he had to make extra sure to shake everything off. A piss in the woods at the nudist resort was extra fast considering he generally didn't need to check if the coast was clear first. Or was it not rude to pee in front of people? He didn't fully understand the culture yet.

Sweat dripped down his stomach and he wiped at it with his hand, matting the thick, dark hair with moisture. He regretted not bringing a towel or something to sit on, but he was tired enough to sit his bare ass on a log. The bark felt dry and hard and like it would leave indentations on his backside the same way he woke up with pillow marks on his face.

He looked down at his socks and shoes. They were the same socks and shoes he had arrived in 2 days ago. He'd figured he didn't need to pack almost anything except his toiletries and antidepressants. It had all fit in his carry-on. When the man next to him on the plane had asked where he was headed, Phillip had pushed himself to say the words "Freedom Resort. It's a nudist thing," because having that kind of vulnerability with a stranger was what this adventure was all about. Challenging himself. Stretching himself. Instead of looking for the perfect partner, BE the perfect partner.

"If you tell a woman that you go to work, come home, play video games, go to sleep, then start all over again, she's not going to be excited to join in your life," his therapist had told him. "You need to have adventures. Do you play video games all weekend too?"

Phillip had been ashamed to say he did.

Now he realized he'd packed too light for this adventure. He had only been thinking about the nudity part of the visit. He hadn't anticipated wanting shower sandals at the pool or boots for hiking. He wore slip-on canvas shoes that were thin enough to feel the larger pieces of detritus he stepped on.

At the sound of sticks breaking under footsteps, Phillip grew somewhat anxious. It could either be a mountain lion come to kill me, he thought, or—and here he shuddered—it could be the Bosmans. The Bosmans were an older couple that boasted a dozen summers at the Freedom Resort in a row. (Mr. Bosman's low-hanging scrotum filled Phillip with dread for the future.) Or what if it was some hiker that wandered onto the property by accident? The website FAQ guaranteed it would be impossible for outsiders to wander onto the resort, but you never knew.

The source of the steps came into view. It was a bipedal, humanoid beast at least seven feet tall. He was covered in fur. When he opened his mouth he unleashed a terrible, guttural grumble. Phillip screamed and fell backwards off his log.

The beast cleared his throat. "Oh, sorry," the beast said in a voice that was unexpectedly friendly. "I didn't mean to scare you, I just haven't spoken in such a long time, it came out all

'Bleghhh!'" The beast waved his hands in a cartoonish mockery of monsters.

"Are you a fucking bigfoot?" Phillip asked, still startled and sprawled in a pile of leaves.

"We prefer sasquatch," he said like a good sport. "And my name is Berf, why not call me that?"

Philip nodded (what else could he really do?) and Berf offered his leathery hand to help him up. He sat down on the log and patted the place next to him so Phillip would join him. Phillip was reluctant but remembered his goal; be adventurous.

"Look, man, I gotta be honest," Berf said. "I thought you were another sasquatch and that's the only reason I came out of my hiding spot. I haven't seen another one of me in like, four winters."

"You thought I was a sasquatch?" Phillip asked.

"Well, maybe like a child sasquatch. I've never seen a human man with so much hair and no clothes on."

Phillip looked down at his body. He was well-aware of his abundant hair. He had to shave his neck, front and back, all the way down to his collarbone and down to the top of his back just so it wouldn't peek out of his t-shirts. Even then, there was obvious stubble left behind and sometimes the hair would peek out anyway. It had been like that since he was sixteen. When he took off his shirt, it looked like he was wearing an angora sweater. The hair thickened around his genitals before thinning out again and reaching every toe.

"It's funny, I guess," Phillip said, used to it by now. "That's what everyone says when I take off my shirt to go swimming or if I'm in the locker room. People feel free, even strangers feel free to comment on my hair, as if I didn't already know."

"Oh, I didn't mean to tease," Berf said, "I mean, what would they say about me in a locker room?"

Phillip studied Berf. His fur was shiny, coated with his natural oils. He could see grayish-brown flesh on Berf's face and nipples, and only in his periphery could he see a penis, the size becoming a beast of his stature. He was too polite to look at it directly, but damn.

"Hey, could I get a hit off that?" Berf said, and motioned to Phillip's water bottle. After a drink, he belched. "God, excuse me, so rude. So why are you out here in the buff anyway?"

"There's a nudist resort a couple of miles down this trail. I'm there for the week. I'm only on my second day," Phillip said, glum as hell.

"Not going so well?" Berf asked.

"It's just not what I expected," Phillip said, realizing how comfortable Berf was making him. "It's a lot of older people that I don't have so much in common with. And then couples. Not a lot of single women, or even single men that I could play some one-on-one with or whatever. And I asked the travel agent ahead of time! I said, Look, I don't want to sound like a creep since it's a nudist resort and everything, but I just want to know that there will be young, single women there. I'm not going there to ogle them or anything, but everyone likes the possibility that they might hook up with someone while they're on vacation."

"That sucks, man," Berf said, nodding his head. "I get it. It's like, even if I run into another sasquatch, there's no guarantee that I'll even get along with them. The last guy I was hanging out with was a terrible companion. He was very young, so maybe he just didn't know better, but he had all these nasty habits. He'd just take a dump wherever and whenever, even if I was right there eating a meal, he'd just squat and keep talking to me like it was nothing. He'd chew at his nails too. Like, I get a twig to dig the dirt out of my nails and I'll file them on a stone, but he's just eating his nails. I ditched him while he was sleeping one night."

"Do you ever meet females?" Phillip asked, "I mean, are you straight?"

"Yes. There was one, Yellyna, and I was in love. I made sure she didn't have to lift a finger. I presented her with armfuls of field mice and berries. I picked the bugs from the fur on her back. But then this guy who was bigger than me came along and her basest instincts kicked in. I told her he wouldn't care for her like I did, but she didn't care. She saw his biceps and just about fainted. Then they were gone."

"I'm so sorry," Phillip said, meaning it.

"But I rarely come across any female sasquatches at all. Are you telling me there's not one single female at this resort?"

"Well, there's one," Phillip said, frowning. "Her name is Jenny. But, I don't know..."

"What?"

"Well, I heard she's divorced. She looks kind of young to be divorced, so what's the story there? There must be something wrong with her, right? And I always pictured myself with someone... I don't know. Different looking from her."

Phillip liked red hair and a long hourglass figure. When he was in high school he had pictures of the lingerie model Ashley Kennedy taped to the walls inside his closet. Jenny was petite with black hair and her dimples and scars hadn't been airbrushed away.

"Have you talked to her, though?" Berf asked.

"No. Just a quick introduction."

"Well, maybe you'd be attracted if you gave it a chance. Maybe the divorce wasn't her fault. Maybe she learned from it. You should talk to her."

"I guess. I just don't want to get her hopes up."

"Get her hopes up? You think she's going wild for this?" Berf said, motioning to Phillip's body, head-to-toe. He was right. Phillip had imagined Jenny being grateful for his attention, but why? She had her own life, her own desires, her own tastes. She didn't need some guy who had been mistaken for a sasquatch by a sasquatch.

"I got waxed once," Phillip said. "My whole chest and stomach and back. Actually didn't hurt as bad as I thought it would. But then it got itchy and it was kind of expensive to do on a monthly basis. It *was* nice to wear a shirt a little unbuttoned at the top, though. I even wore a v-neck."

"Maybe you should just accept your body and decide that it's beautiful instead of trying to change it. Confidence is sexy," Berf said. "And you can't love others until you love yourself."

"How do you know so much about humans?"

"I sneak into people's vacation homes and watch TV. It's tough to get in and out without being seen, but it's kind of adventurous, like I'm on a mission. I love the look on someone's face when they see me, then they start scrambling to get their camera out and poof, I'm gone."

Phillip laughed. He stood up and stretched. He brushed pine needles off his ass cheeks.

"I should head back. Thanks for the insight. I was being kind of a jerk. Love comes when you least expect it, right?"

When Phillip looked back down at the log, Berf was gone.

"Hey! I wanted to ask- if you guys exist, why don't we find any skeletal remains?!" Phillip shouted, "Hello?"

No answer.

He hiked back to the resort. People seem to like Jenny, he thought, there must be a good reason.

12

BILLY'S MEMOIR, 2020

Dear Family,

Another message from your now famous bestselling son/brother/nephew/cousin! Exciting, right?

An update since the last time I wrote: Mittens is dead. She ate an entire pack of cigarettes which I had left out on a counter. I had no idea it was such a hazard, but I needed the cigarettes to write my memoir.

And that's why I'm writing you today. The memoir! When no one was willing to share their inheritance with me, I had to find a way to earn an honest living (you lazy bums! ;)), so I wrote a memoir.

I received your messages, by the way. I understand some of you aren't happy with the way you were portrayed in my book and to that I say, you *who*? I changed everyone's names. Gare Bear, I know you think you're Grady, but I can neither confirm nor deny that. Gwyn, you probably think you're Guadalupe, but that's obviously not your name.

Mom and Dad, do I even have to justify myself? I called you "Mom and Dad" in the book, so no one even knows your names. There's at least a million "Mom and Dads" in the world.

Yes, I included some family photos, but we all look so different now. So much *older*. *Wiser*. More harmonious! Comfortable with ourselves and our pasts.

But let's break down some of the passages you take issue with.

Dad took a short break from his workaholism to come down to the lake and drive the boat so we could waterski. It wasn't often that I saw him without a shirt on, even on vacation he wore button-downs, but that day he went topless and the pattern of his chest hair reminded me of a scientific illustration of the female reproductive system.

Grady was, as usual, overconfident and clueless. He wanted to ski without a life vest on. Mom was busy drinking her fifth gimlet of the day and reading a ghoulish Anne Rule book, so she was completely checked out. Dad, because of his lack of presence, assumed Grady could swim just fine, so he said nothing.

"Don't do it, Grady," I said. "You could drown! Mom! Dad! Don't let him do it!"

"Shut the fuck up, son," Dad said through the cigar planted between his molars.

I anxiously anticipated Grady's drowning and steeled myself to save him. He squeezed his feet into the water skis and arranged his body in the water like a woman awaiting a pap smear.

"Go!" he shouted.

Under Dad's governance, the boat lurched forward, sped towards the center of the lake and turned sharply. Not much of an athlete, Grady was only up on the skis for about eight seconds, but it felt like even less. He lost his grip on the rope and toppled end-over-end and into the depths of the lake.

"Stop!" I shouted at my father, suddenly realizing how much I wanted Grady to live.

Dad came to a halt and I dove into the water like a father dolphin and swam with all my might towards my beloved brother. He was sputtering and flailing his limbs. His head bobbed above and below the surface of the murky water over and over.

"It's gonna be ok," I shouted as I put one arm around him and side-stroked my way back to the boat. Dad helped pull him back in.

"Get in the boat, goddammit!" he said.

Grady was still struggling to breathe and Dad slapped his back, but I was the one who eased Grady to the floor of the boat and performed mouth-to-mouth.

A gush of water bubbled up and he could breathe again. As soon as he finished coughing, he spoke.

"Why'd you pull me out of the water, Billy?! I was fine! Geez! You ruined my turn at skiing! Dad, give me Billy's turn!"

"You can have my turn, I'm just so glad you're safe," I said.

* * *

OK, let me clue you in on something about writing memoirs. You have to be honest about what happened, but you're allowed to change small details, both to protect identities and to add some drama.

That story happened! Who cares if I was the one who nearly drowned and Gare Bear was the one who saved me. (Let's be honest, though, between the five of us, I was a great swimmer and I would have been fine. Gare Bear, I know you think you saved my life, but did you?)

As for the exact number of gimlets Mom drank, I don't know, but five was probably close. And you did love Anne Rule, Mom. Admit it.

And Dad, your attitude in the story was impressionistic.

Those weren't exact quotes, but I *feel* that that was what you were thinking.

Another passage you've disputed-

Two things were clear: Guadalupe's marriage was in trouble and Christmas brought out the worst in my family.

Stick-thin and a raw foodist, I had never seen Guadalupe gulp down something as "toxic" as wassail spiked with whiskey. When I saw that she was becoming drunk, I tucked her kids into bed for her. It was Christmas Eve, so I read The Night Before Christmas to them.

"Uncle Billy, can you be our Dad?"

It broke my heart to witness their clear instability and disgusting ideas about me having an incestuous relationship with their mother. You have to wonder where they picked up that twisted idea.

They grew up in a spotlight, the paparazzi sometimes photographing them out with their father. He should have done more to protect them.

I kissed them each on the head and said goodnight before returning to Guadalupe. She was in front of the fire, alone, and adding more whiskey to her cup. She had started with the good stuff, but was now on to Seagrams; like a couple that begins their affair at The Four Seasons and ends it in the back of a Corolla.

"I think he's having an affair with this total whore actress who is starring in a romantic comedy with him that is coming out March 2022."

That is when, I humbly admit, I made a mistake. I opted for some tough love.

"You kind of knew what you were getting into when you married him, didn't you? God, why did I say that. I'm sorry. I shouldn't have blamed the victim. Tell me more. What is he like at home?"

"Gross. You should see his feet. He has fungus. His toenails are

yellow and brittle. I have scratches on my legs from when they rub up against me in bed. He has night terrors. I wake up to him screaming, flailing in bed with his toenails cutting my legs. Whatever. His total whore actress girlfriend who is starring in a romantic comedy with him that comes out March 2022 can have him."

I protected all identities and if there was a spike in Tom's IMDB views on the day my book came out, I certainly can't help it. Maybe it's a coincidence. The tabloids can talk all they want, but they won't receive any confirmation, so that's all it is: talk!

And who is Guadalupe anyway?

I know there are a lot of contentious passages, but I only have time to discuss one more.

My mother's obsessions with true crime and occult stories took an even darker turn. She held a seance in our home. A few of her friends came over for a "book club", I saw our Ouija board sitting on a shelf in the living room, and I put two and two together. They were supposedly discussing a book called Memories of Midnight the whole time, but they must have been speaking in code. Her father was the leader of a satanic cult, so it ran in her blood and, unfortunately, mine. I was strong enough to resist that darkness, but alas, she was not.

I went to bed alone, and afraid. No one to read me a story or to make sure that I brushed my teeth.

I awoke, startled, around midnight. Mom was hovering over me, reeking of Chardonnay, bringing her hand towards my neck with a blanket clutched in it. I saw a silver glint near her other hand. The kind of glint you might see on a dagger.

"Mom? What's happening?" I asked.

Her eyes, normally brown, darkened as she tightened her grip on what might have been a ceremonial dagger.

"It's over," she said softly.

Was she referring to her seance, or my life? Could she be referring to the end of humanity and a coming antichrist? Only she knows.

I quickly fell back asleep, possibly by being overcome by chloroform.

When I awoke, I thanked God for sparing me and decided to dedicate my life to doing good.

Mom, you may not be proud of this moment and I know that you love me. You lost your way for a while and it can be painful to confront that, but the truth is the truth.

And no one knows who any of you are for sure anyway, except my friends and our family and anyone who found that genealogy Grandma wrote.

If there are any other passages that any of you feel you need to talk through, let's do it. It'll be like online family therapy. How refreshing!

I do have a gripe of my own, though. I expected a little more support, perhaps a "Congratulations, Billy!" after my breakout debut as a writer. I forgive you in advance. I trust that the commendation will come in due time.

Headed to Tokyo next week as part of my book tour. Will pick up souvenirs.

With Great Respect,

Billy

13

———

BILLY'S MINI-SERIES, 2021

Dear Family,

I haven't heard much from any of you, at least not directly. I've been getting on fabulously with your lawyers. It almost got ugly there for a moment, but I smoothed things over. That's always been my role in the family.

I'm writing because, as you may have heard, my memoir has been optioned for a mini-series! The screenwriter wanted to see if any of you remembered additional details about a few passages. Here are a few off the top of my head.

———

As a teen, Guadalupe became moody and took to writing poetry in her diary. She was too modest to share it, so I, her loving little brother, took the liberty of reading the poems and marking them with red pen so she could improve them. She was angry. Not everyone accepts criticism well, but she eventually came to think of it as one of her earliest lessons in writing. Who knows where she would be if I hadn't studied such a great deal of Shel Silverstein, read her diary, and dug out a red pen from her school bag?

When she published her first poetry collection in her twenties, she dedicated it to me. I was with her when she drafted the dedication.

"To my brother Billy who encouraged me from the start.

B is for benevolent,

I is for intelligent..."

"Stop," I said. "An acrostic poem? It's juvenile. Be better than this."

At this point, she was no longer threatened by my criticism. It only spurred her on. She changed it.

"To my brother Billy, you're my favorite person in the world and I couldn't have written this book without you."

Always the editor, I gave her one more piece of feedback.

"Don't dedicate it to me," I said. "Because that will be all the thanks I get. If I can manage to be your hero in private and without fanfare, I'll receive treasures in heaven."

"As you wish," she said. She backspaced the dedication away and replaced it with the one you see in the book today.

"To the man who inspired so many of these poems, I love you."

Most people assume the "man" is her charismatic husband Tom, but I know who it really is.

It's me.

She told me it's about Tom, but there always seems to be a subtle wink in her eye when she says it.

So, Gwyn, I know you may not remember this exchange, you might even say that I made it up full cloth, but I remember it like it was yesterday. And it could be such a great little moment in the mini-series! I hope you'll confirm this story even if you don't remember it. If it turns out the "man" you were dedicating your book to *is* actually your (estranged) husband, perhaps we can revise history since you're separated from him now. Do you really want to be associated with that cheating bastard?

Gare Bear, they may be asking about medical records for this story:

When I was nineteen and studying Biology, I had a little bachelor pad off campus where I enjoyed hosting dinner parties and, yes, brought women home so I could help them connect with their feminine sensuality.

Grady knocked on my door one Saturday, and thankfully, I was alone that particular morning.

"Billy, I screwed up! I screwed up really bad!" He cried in a panic, barely able to catch his breath. I slapped him across the face to sober him up. He put his hand to his cheek and slowed his breath. I guided him to the couch and brought him a glass of water.

"Drink!" I said.

He smelled of bodily fluids and booze. He had graduated two years prior, but he hadn't stopped partying. Grady had turned into the weird guy still hanging around frat parties with guys he barely knew while all his friends had moved on.

"What happened?" I asked.

"I woke up in my bed with a bloody hammer in my hand," he stammered. "There's hair stuck to the blood. I don't know where it came from or what I did. I don't even remember getting home last night."

I questioned him with the calmness and reason a 911 operator might possess.

"Was there blood in your bed?"

"No. I don't know. Maybe?"

"Where's the hammer?"

"I dropped it on the bedroom floor."

"Let's check the news."

I fired up my laptop and searched for any news about gruesome murders in the area. I found nothing.

Then I saw the dried blood at the edge of his baseball cap. I lifted the cap, revealing his receding hairline (expected) and a wound on his head (unexpected).

"Holy shit, Grady, you hit your own head with a hammer!"

He felt his head and saw the blood on his hand.

"I thought the pain was just a hangover!" he said, gingerly fingering the wound and recoiling from the sensitivity.

I retrieved my first aid kit. I cleaned the wound and gave him five stitches. Goddamn if I shouldn't have become a doctor. My professors all told me I'd shine in an operating room, but I foolishly dropped out. I'm too free a spirit.

Grady thanked me for talking him back down.

"You should quit partying and get your life together. Didn't you want to start a business?" I asked him.

That day, Grady stopped drinking and started the business that became the successful corporation it is today, Crantran Corp.

And it's all because I gave him a few stitches and told him to get his act together. He couldn't have done it without me.

Gare Bear, you'd have a good **excuse** for not remembering this because of your head injury. Do you still have that scar on your head? I bet the hair just grew right back over it unless that part of your head is totally bald now. I did a pretty tidy job on those stitches. Anyway, if you don't remember, just tell them to trust me and that you don't have any more details to add.

I know, my book protected your identities, but they're taking the reality of it so seriously. Kind of lame. Like, this isn't a documentary!

OK, one more they might wonder about.

I've been very open about how distant my Dad was most of the time. When I tell people this, sometimes they ask me if he ever gave me a sex talk.

He did.

Unfortunately, he gave me this talk while drunk or high on cocaine, or both.

It was confusing and to this day, I question whether he knows how reproduction works. He's a brilliant businessman, but science escapes him. I'll do my best to replicate what he said to me.

"A woman is born with all the babies inside her nuts that she's ever going to have. Each has a name and personality, and some are even differently abled. Women all have a couple of conjoined twins in there too. The one thing the babies are missing is a soul, which comes from the man.

Once a month, a baby (or a set of conjoined twins) shakes loose from her nuts like apples falling from a tree. See, Billy, the inside of a woman's body is shaped like a funnel and the babies flow out of her— yes, even your sister. Anyway. Those monthly babies are tiny, so she can't see them and it's not a big deal, especially since they didn't have souls yet.

If a woman lets you put a soul in her, it will flow out of your bone hole, snake its way up to her funnel and swallow up one of the babies. Now that it has a soul, it can grow into its final form.

You'll want to leave a woman alone as the baby grows because a baby is delicate and because she'll be in a bad mood and complain about back pain a lot. Then she'll complain that you aren't being supportive and you'll have to hire someone to support her.

When she gives birth, you'll catch the slimy, gray baby, hold it one time for a photo, and then put it down and never pick it back up again. At some point, you'll tell them about sex, pay for stuff including college and a wedding, and then they'll care for you when you're old or else dump you in some nursing home. Circle of life."

I think he may have been under extreme stress at work. I can only speculate. Perhaps he committed fraud or embezzlement. Perhaps he had a sexual harassment scandal. Being under that sort of pressure does funny things to our minds.

Dad, I was very young when you said this to me, so I may not have remembered it with complete accuracy, but you definitely used the words "sex," "baby," and "nuts."

Well, I gave the screenwriter your phone numbers, so think of more details if you can, but if you can't, that's ok.

(Not that these stories are about you, LOL.)

Gotta get back to work on my second memoir. Even though my first one made enough to cover all of my lawsuits and leave behind some spending cash, I have a feeling I might need more. That's why I optioned the story for the series and should have another book out next year.

Billy

14

THE GOOD SAMARITAN OF SILVERLAKE, 2005

"Hey man, are you ok?"

The cyclist was lying on the street with the good samaritan squatting beside him. A car slowly curved around both of them.

"No!" the cyclist groaned. "It hurts too bad to get up."

They were on Sunset Boulevard in front of a row of restaurants and boutiques patronized by hipsters and the occasional B-list celebrity.

"My friend is calling for an ambulance right now," the Samaritan said calmly. "She's still at the table. We were in the middle of lunch when you were hit by that car. They drove away too, jerks. My friend and I were meeting up to talk about a short film idea. Actually, it's little thriller about an illuminati cult in a quaint suburb of Seattle. Basically, it starts when--"

"Aaaagh, my back!" the cyclist cried.

"Help is on the way! You really should have been wearing a helmet. I see you're wearing a beanie, but that's not going to do much if you have an accident. *Right now*, for instance. Also, it's 85 degrees out. Aren't you hot in that beanie? Helmets have holes in the top so heat can escape."

"Am I bleeding anywhere?" the cyclist asked.

"I don't see any blood. Well, your arm is scraped up, but it's not like, *bleeding* bleeding. Is it a vanity thing? Is that why you didn't wear a helmet? Because it looks lame? You look like a stylish guy. Your bike is cool, too. Bummer it's so banged up now. I've been toying with the idea of getting a bike, but now I'm not sure. I probably wouldn't want to wear a helmet either. My hair is really thick and when you disturb the product it turns frizzy. See?"

"It hurts!" he said, and gripped the knee of his torn jeans.

"I wish there was more I could do for you, but honestly, I have no idea how to help you. I wish I could do more. Damn, my food just arrived at the table. I ordered the fish tacos. Have you ever had them here? They're topped with local slaw. They're so good, that I haven't even tried anything else on the menu. And the other stuff looks really good. Like, they have a jackfruit curry which sounds amazing. But the fish tacos.... Mmm."

"Where's the ambulance?" the cyclist said between gritted teeth. He didn't seem to care too much about jackfruit curry, or fish tacos, even.

"Let me check," the good samaritan said. "Hey, Lucy! Did they say how long?"

"The food is already here!" Lucy called back.

"No, not the food. How long til the *ambulance* is here?"

"They didn't tell me!" Lucy said through a mouthful of jackfruit.

"Dang. She's eating without me. She got the curry. I mean, I don't want her food to get cold. She should enjoy it. It's just a bummer that by the time I'm eating, she's just going to be sitting there watching me eat and I'll feel rushed."

The good samaritan steadied himself by putting his knuckles down on the street, and then immediately withdrew them. The cyclist was writhing, arching his back to get it away from the hot asphalt, then hunching to get his shoulders and ass away from it.

"Wow! The pavement is friggin' hot. Isn't it burning your skin?" He said, blowing on his hand.

"Yes!"

"Hey, I think I hear the ambulance? Do you hear it?"

"Aghhhh!" the cyclist cried out. He continued to experiment with bodily positions but everything he did either burned him or exacerbated his injuries.

"No wait, that was a police siren. I don't hear it anymore, they must be driving away from us. False alarm! No wait, it *was* the ambulance! Here they come! I'll wave at them."

"Oh thank god. It hurts," the cyclist moaned, though it wasn't clear whether he meant his body or his present company.

"I'll stay with you until they're here. I'm taking a screenwriting course and this would be really interesting to write about. I mean, if this was a movie, what do you think would happen next? Maybe we'd become roommates so I could nurse you back to health while I build a special tandem bike to take you out on rides and we'd be lifelong friends."

"Oh dear god."

"Well, here they are. Gotta jet and eat those tacos before they get soggy from the local slaw. I just gotta say, being by your side in your dark moment has been a hell of an experience for me and I hope you recover quickly. Good luck! And get a helmet, ok?"

The good samaritan returned to their table. The server refilled their cucumber water.

"I took the fish tacos off your bill," the server said, "You're a hero, helping that guy! I wouldn't have known what to do."

"It's just my duty as a human," the good samaritan said, "Someone has to step up. Might as well be me."

The good samaritan bit into a taco and tasted the satisfaction of having a pure heart.

15

A NOTE ON YOUR WINDSHIELD, 2005

To whom it may concern (ahem, maroon honda):

I was about to write you a note to tell you that you park like an asshole, but I had a change of heart. I don't know your circumstances. Maybe you were in a hurry because you had to get to a bathroom. Maybe you were distracted by the pain of spilling an americano in your lap. Who am I to judge?

I once received a note on my windshield. The note said: "I hit your car. There are people watching. I'm pretending to write a note with my contact info."

Well that really ruined my day. You want to believe there are good people in the world. So here I am being a good person. I was going to write you a nasty note, but I didn't want to ruin your day. The problem is, if I don't write a note to let you know that I thought about writing a nasty note, then decided not to, you wouldn't know that someone did something nice for you! So now you know there are good people in the world. Me!

I just noticed that you have a little Catholic thingy hanging on your rear view mirror. If you're going to show the world that you're Catholic, guess what? You now represent all Catholics. If you park in such a way that you take two spots, people are going to think all Catholics park like assholes. In my humble opinion, you ought to take down the thingy if you're going to do a bad job of parking. That way, people don't think bad stuff about your people. OR—and this is the better option—resolve to always do a good job of parking no matter what.

Do you think they ever park the pope-mobile in such a way that they take up two spaces? I doubt it. They're probably very conscientious because they don't want people thinking the pope is some kind of jerk.

Now that I look past the Catholic thingy, there's a lot of stuff in your car. Kind of messy. Did you know it takes twenty-eight days to form a habit? For twenty-eight days, I took my car to the wash once a week and always used that vacuum on my interior. Using the vacuum forced me to throw out the old cups, napkins, and cologne samples that are always falling into the seat crack. The reason I started that habit was because I picked up a woman for a date once and she looked a little grossed out by my car. There were some cold, stiff french fries around her feet and my gym bag didn't exactly smell like pansies. She didn't see me again after that.

I see a yoga mat in the back seat so there's an 80% chance you're female. I went to a class once and felt like everyone thought I was there to creep on women. There were only like, two other guys in the class. One of them was *really* good at yoga. I knew he was going to be good because he wore these tiny little yoga shorts and nothing else. Why would someone wear that unless they were really good at yoga? And the other guy in the class had on sweats and started off doing yoga in sneakers, then partway through realized everyone else was barefoot. He stopped and took his sneakers off.

I bet *he* was there to creep on women.

I was just there to do yoga and meet new people. I met a woman named Sabrina and asked her to meet up some time, but she said she felt uncomfortable giving her number out to a guy she just met after yoga. I told her we could just go out as friends and she still said no as if I was some kind of yoga creep. She ruined my day just like the guy who put the note on my windshield. I don't want to be the kind of person who ruins someone else's day. That's why I'm trying not to be judgmental about your parking. You probably had a good reason to take up two parking spaces.

It's possible you didn't though. If you didn't have a good reason to park this way, well then, you park like an asshole.

I hope I brightened your day! Namaste.

16

A NOTE ABOUT YOUR BIKE, 2005

Dear Person Whose Bike Was Chained to This Pole -

You're lucky I was around because I am on an absolute tear of good deeds. I was just walking home from the pharmacy when I saw this guy look around, get a bolt cutter out of his back pack, and start working away at your bike chain. He didn't notice me coming because he was so focused. I hid behind the apartment building's dumpster to watch what he did.

He was a skinny white guy, early twenties. Didn't look like a crackhead or anything, just like a young guy. He looked like a musician actually. He was kind of cool in a don't-give-a-shit way.

Anyway, he was working at your chain and I started to wonder if I should stop him. Calling the police probably wouldn't do. It would take them too long to get here. And what if he had a knife or something? I decided that my best bet was not to come in like a tough guy, but more like a concerned citizen. An innocent bystander!

I started walking towards him and he saw me but acted casual.

"Hey man, you know a key would work better on that?" I said.

"Lost my key," he said, chuckling lightly.

"Oh, that's funny..." I said, really clever now, "because the lock is code based! There never was a key! You're stealing this bike, aren't you?"

"I know it's code based. I was just going along with your dumb joke to be nice."

He got me there. I expected a confession but didn't get one.

"So, why don't you use the code?"

"I forgot the code," he said, beginning to speed up, working away at the chain as fast as his skinny little arms could. He was grunting and everything.

"I guess you won't mind if I take your picture, then," I said.

I got my camera phone out and pointed it at him. He lowered his hat over his face, but I still took a picture.

"Dude, I'm not stealing a bike, it's my bike!" he said. "You're harassing me. I should be taking a photo of you!"

Clever, right? This kid was the master of manipulation, but he didn't realize who he was dealing with.

"I'm happy for you to take a picture of me. Go ahead!" I said. I smoothed out my hair for a picture. He didn't do it. I think he was a little afraid of me. And maybe he didn't have a camera phone.

I took a second picture of the tattoo of a star on his wrist and figured that was enough evidence. I needed my hands free to physically defend myself if it came to fisticuffs.

He finally got through the lock and worked quickly to untangle it from the bike. I picked up a big stick on the sly and when he went to ride away, I shoved the stick into the spokes. He jerked, lost his balance, and fell off just enough for me to grab the bike and speed away. He couldn't keep up with me on foot and I quickly lost him!

I rode all the way home, honestly really proud of myself for saving your bike. So, the bike is at my house now.

Here's the catch: I'm moving today. The movers are loading the truck RIGHT NOW. So, you have to come get your bike in the next hour or two. If you don't, I could just leave it outside, but I don't have a lock and obviously someone would steal it. So, if you don't come get it, I'll just take it with me. I figured you'd rather *me* have it than some random thieving punk, right?

I'm the brick apartment building on 10th and Hazelnut.

Hope you get this message and get to my place soon! If you don't make it, you should do a fundraiser to get a new bike. Those seem to work really well.

Stay cool!

-The Bike Saver

Ps: I'll send the photo to the police, but it'll have to be anonymous because I have an unpaid parking ticket.

17

I, PUBESCENT, 1999

I trip on a crack in the sidewalk on my way up to the evilest house in the neighborhood to save people from going to hell. I read that people my age trip a lot because our feet grow faster than the rest of our body and we're not used to it yet. I think I read it in *Brio*.

Stupid shirt. I ran out of black t-shirts to wear because Mom forgot to do laundry. My shirt is tight and pink, but because of my sweat problem, the pits are magenta. I normally wear black and keep my arms down tight so the pit stains don't show. The reason I especially have a sweat problem is 'cause I wear a back brace for twenty-three hours a day so that makes me even hotter, but my Mom says it's hormones.

I should have worn shorts, too. My jeans feel drenched, but at least the stickiness is keeping my jeans from riding down and showing my butt crack, so that's good.

I wipe the sweat from my forehead, which you can see a lot of because my friend said she knew how to cut bangs and then she cut mine way too short. She paired off with someone else to share Jesus with because she was avoiding me because she knows she made my bangs look stumpy and my face look like the moon. Everyone else got to knock on doors in pairs, but there was an odd number. I thought it made sense to go in a group of three, but everyone said we'd cover more houses if I went by myself. Save more people from hell. They told me to get out of my comfort zone.

So I am.

They're going to regular houses. I'm going to the one where I heard they have a satanic cult dungeon. It's the biggest house with the biggest yard. I heard a developer wanted to buy their property but the people who live there didn't want to move because they have a secret dungeon they don't want anyone to know about.

The walk is taking longer than I thought.

Someone will probably kidnap me because even though I'm thirteen and going to high school in the fall people think I'm younger, always. It's because I'm short and my chest is still pretty flat. I have round cheeks too. And here I am alone. My church is going to feel *so bad* if I get kidnapped. They'll hold a prayer-athon like they did when Mr. Zandstra had his prostate out.

There's a wrought iron fence around the whole place, but the gate is open. I trip again on the porch steps, push my glasses back up because my sweaty nose let them slide down, and knock lightly because I kind of hope no one answers. The pamphlet I brought is getting wavy from all the sweat on my hands. I hear footsteps coming and get a little bit nervous.

The door opens and I hope there will be a whoosh of cold air like when you walk into a grocery store. Instead, I think the house is swallowing the heat. A boy is standing there.

"'Sup?" he says.

He looks like he's probably in high school, but older high school. He's wearing basketball shorts and no shirt and he has muscles showing. He looks like he's probably popular and could be smoking weed and frenching in someone's basement with no parents home. My face turns red.

"Hi," I say, and search my mind for our script. "Do you feel confident that if you died today you'd go to heaven?"

"I don't really believe in heaven," he says.

I open the tract to show the illustration of the canyon just like we were taught.

"If a bunch of people tried to jump across the Grand Canyon, and like, heaven is on the other side, some people might get further than others, but no one is going to make it. No one is good enough."

I turn the page. A big cross bridges the gap across the canyon. It says JESUS on the cross.

"That's why we all need Jesus. No one is pure enough to be in God's presence, but Jesus washes our sins away. He is the only way to heaven."

"So then you walk across the cross to get from one side of the Grand Canyon to heaven? Is heaven in Arizona?"

"Close the door! You're letting the air out," a woman calls from inside the house.

"Wanna come inside?" he says, and because I'm desperate for cool air and I know a woman, probably his mom, is there, I do it. I'm not supposed to be alone with boys.

I smell body odor and don't know if it's him or me. I mean, I'm the one sweating a lot, but he's the one not wearing a shirt so his actual pits are showing. I almost sniff my pits, but stop myself because that would be so stupid.

"Let me get you some water," he says and disappears. Somewhere in the house a radio is playing the same radio show that my mom listens to on Saturday mornings. It's a quiz show on NPR where everyone is always laughing about nothing. Like, literally, everything anyone says is a little joke that only people over forty understand.

He returns with a plastic bottle of water for me.

"Thanks," I say, and take a drink. The opening makes an audible clack against my braces.

"So, the cross is a bridge, but when you're walking across it, what about the middle part of the cross that sticks up. How do you get up and over that part? Is there like a grappling hook that represents good deeds?"

I want to leave because I feel like he's teasing me. I feel dumb and I don't know how to end this conversation—they didn't prepare us for this question—but I'm still so thankful for the water and the air conditioner and I really want to save the satanists.

"Kidding," he says. "I'm Billy, by the way. Have you ever actually converted someone by knocking on their door?"

"I'm Hannah. And no, I haven't," I say. In fact, no one in my youth group has converted someone by knocking on a door, but they told us that being persecuted means you're doing something right.

"Most people in the US know what Christianity is, anyhow," says Billy. "If I was interested, I'd join a church. I'm just trying to keep you from wasting your time. I mean, your plan probably isn't going to work."

"It's not *my* plan," I say.

"Whose plan is it?"

"Pastor Brandon."

"And he's making you do this?" he asks.

"Well, not *making*. But I'm supposed to do it. And I don't want people to go to Hell." I drink more water and notice a crucifix on the wall. "Is your grandma catholic?"

He says yes and I peer around to see if we're alone. Since he's close to my age, I feel like I can ask and he won't think it's rude. I can't believe I'm in the house I've been warned about for years and it would be crazy *not* to get the truth.

"Do you know the rumors about your grandparents?" I ask.

"I have a feeling I know, but I'd like to hear them anyway," Billy says, smiling like he's enjoying talking to me.

I say it as quietly as I can because I'm scared if his grandparents hear me they'll try to curse me and even though Jesus is stronger than any curse, a curse would probably still suck at least for a little while.

"Everyone says that your grandparents are satanists and that they have a satanic cult that meets in a secret dungeon under this house."

"We don't really talk about it," Billy says.

He's speaking quietly too and I think he's being serious. I don't think he's joking with me. He doesn't seem to be afraid, though.

"Have you ever been in the dungeon?" I whisper.

"No. But last night my gramp went out back and he was gone for a long time and I wasn't sure what he was doing back there," Billy said. He leaned in closer and smiled. "Hey, why don't you come back after dark and we'll see if we can find the entrance?"

My heart speeds. Pastor Brandon and my parents would tell me not to do it, but I feel God telling me that I could take down this whole operation if I could just stand in that dungeon and pray over it.

"Ok," I say. "Do you want to keep the tract?"

I hold it out and immediately regret it since it's so wet from my sweaty hand. He takes it. He was probably prom king or something and now he's holding my sweaty Jesus pamphlet and he knows my name. He's probably had sex! And I think it's probably me that smells.

He reaches past me for the front door. He smells like body spray. I can't wait to see him smile again.

"Tonight. 10pm. Meet me by the gate," he says before closing the door.

I linger on the porch in the shade and take another sip of water. Across the street I see two of my friends being confronted by a man who is pointing to his "No Soliciting" sign.

"We're not selling anything," I think I hear them say.

I feel like I've done my duty, so I'm just going to stand here a while. I'll tell them my back hurt. They're not going to believe I came to this house. They're going to feel so bad if I get demon possessed.

Anyway, I can't think about Jesus right now. All I can think about is Billy with no shirt on who smells like body spray. He'd look cute getting baptized.

My parents are surprised when I go to bed early like them. During the summer I usually stay up late to watch movies I checked out from the library. The librarian doesn't care if I check out rated R movies, but I have to watch them with the volume low so my parents don't hear the f-word.

Sneaking out isn't hard. I pile my stuffed animals under my blanket so they look a little like a sleeping body if you squint. Then I just walk out the back door. I did laundry so I could wear black and I leave my back brace at home in case I need to be flexible. I pray during my walk to the Satanic house that God would protect me.

Billy is by the gate, and he's smoking a cigarette.

"You shouldn't smoke," I say, "You can get addicted and it gives you cancer."

"I'll quit someday. You wanna try it?" he asks.

"Totally," I say.

I suck on the cigarette and start coughing like crazy. Billy laughs at me, but not in a mean way. He tosses the cigarette onto the sidewalk and beckons me to the yard. I stomp out the cigarette first because it's been dry out, but then I follow.

He leads me to a cellar door surrounded by shrubs at the back of the house. The padlock that had been holding it shut is on the ground.

"Why is it unlocked?" I ask.

"I don't know," he says, "I found it this way. We have to open and close it quietly, though. You go first."

He lifts the door and I can see one wood step. The rest is darkness.

"No. You go first," I say.

He nods and uses his lighter to see where he's going. I pick up the padlock to take with us so no one can lock us in. He closes the door gently.

There's no lamps, just candles. Billy opens a refrigerator to light the room.

"Fuckin' sweet," he says. He takes a sword down from the wall.

"I have to pee," I say. Just like when I was a kid playing Hide-and-go-seek. I would hide and suddenly have to pee because I was so nervous.

He points the sword to the corner.

"I think that might be a bathroom."

I enter the small room and find that there's a light switch and, thankfully, a toilet. I close the door and go. It's impossible for my pee to not be noisy. It's so quiet in the dungeon.

Just after pulling up my pants, Billy opens the door without knocking and says someone's coming. I start to hyperventilate.

"The satanists are coming!" I say.

"Shhhh!" he says, "If we get caught, it's just my grandparents. They're not going to kill us or anything."

"But I'm a virgin!" I say, "They're going to sacrifice me!"

"I won't let them," Billy says, cupping my face with his

hands, "You have to be quiet though and we just have to hope they don't come in here."

Footsteps descend. Two people.

"All right, Tim, what was so important that it couldn't wait until our next mass," the first voice says. I think it's his grandpa.

"I just had a couple ideas I wanted to bounce off of you."

I hear the sound of a match being lit. Billy and I are huddled together and this Tim guy is talking about going on a retreat with a ropes course.

"They're not doing anything bad," Billy whispers. "It's just a silly club."

"Couldn't we just have spoken on the phone?" Billy's grandpa says. He sounds annoyed.

"I guess," says the man he called Tim. "But I didn't want to ask in front of everyone else because Pete keeps trying to take credit for my ideas."

"I'm missing a re-run of *Frasier!*" Billy's Grandpa says.

"Have you ever kissed anyone?" Billy whispers to me.

I'm thankful he can't see me blush.

"No. Have you?"

"Yeah. Lots of girls. They've told me I'm good at it. Do you want me to kiss you? It'll feel really good."

I nod. Lightning-fast, I worry about the moisture level of my lips and my breath and whether I'm going to do it right, so I just sit still and let him do it.

It's like fireworks explode in my body.

I think he might be The One, but how could he be? He's going to go to Hell when he dies.

"Billy, I'm really sorry, but you can't be my boyfriend," I say.

"Cool," he says.

Thank God I didn't break his heart too badly.

It became quiet in the dungeon.

"Are they gone?" I whisper.

The bathroom door suddenly swings open. Billy's grandpa with his bushy white eyebrows and sharp face scowls at us.

"What the devil are you doing in here?" he asks.

"The power of Christ compels you!" I shout.

The Exorcist gave me nightmares, but in this moment I'm thankful the library let me check it out.

I grab Billy's hand and run. I push his grandpa to the side, haul ass up the steps, and burst forth from the cellar doors. Even when I let go of his hand, he runs with me all the way to the sidewalk.

"That was fun!" he says.

"Don't tell him my name!" I say. This must be what a heart attack feels like. "Don't tell him anything about me!"

"Ok," Billy says, "I'll just tell him we snuck down there to make out."

"Are you going to be in trouble?"

"It'll be fine," Billy says. "My grandpa will be mad. My grandma used to be nice, but she's gotten kind of mean as she's gotten older, but what are they going to do? Yell a little? No big whoop."

"You won't see me again," I say. "Kiss me goodbye."

He kisses me longer and harder than the first time. When he releases me, I run all the way home as fast as my scoliosis will allow. I think I hear him laughing, but not in a mean way.

I don't get caught, but even if I did, it would be worth it. I may have just brought down a satanic cult with the power of Christ.

18

MARKETING A ROBO-DUD, 2031

"There have been complaints about the Somebot Model 30 making people uncomfortable, but Somebot doesn't want to scrap it because then they'd be out billions of dollars," Jon said. He leaned his elbows onto the knees of his I-don't-give-a-shit ripped jeans.

"Who did the first campaign?" Constance asked.

"Planet B. and their marketing strategy was basically: "look how humanlike this is.""

"And that's what people hate about it," Babs said, "It's what I hate about it, for sure."

"Oh, yeah, I forgot you had one," Constance said.

Babs' dog jumped into her lap. The three sat in a throwback 1970s conversation pit—a feature all the tech and marketing firms were adding to their offices lately. Bonus points if you had some antique owl decorations, but they were difficult to find.

Constance tried to beckon Babs' dog towards her, but he wouldn't budge. Babs and her dog had the same blonde curls and mild disposition. The dog even had a human-like face that elicited Constance's affection.

"Is there anything you *do* like about it?" Jon asked.

"I like almost everything about what it does," Babs said. "It preps all my veggies before I cook. It keeps the whole house pretty clean as long as I pick up my own clutter. It walks Sweet Puppers. And it' does it all better than the original Somebot. It's just that..."

Babs cringed. Jon and Constance understood and mirrored her grimace.

"I feel like there's actually someone in my house. Even if I go in my bedroom and close the door. I think about the Model 30 sitting on its power hub and... this is going to sound crazy, but I worry that it's bored. Because it looks so human, I assign human feelings to it and I worry that it feels like a slave. And then, let's say the singularity *did* happen," Babs said, her eyes going wide. "It would probably hate me. I've been having it file my corns every night!"

Constance grimaced at the thought of corns being scraped away by a grotesque caricature of a human.

"I was at a friend's house and was greeted at the door by her Model 30," she said. "I felt like I had to be polite to it and make small talk. I couldn't relax."

"Exactly!" Babs said. "I can't relax in my own home. I don't like singing in front of people, but I used to sing in my kitchen while I cooked. Now I don't because I'm afraid I'm annoying it and I'm embarrassed about my voice."

"So, we either have to convince people not to feel weird and self-conscious around the Model 30, or... what else?" Jon asked. They sat in silence for a few minutes until Constance spoke up, excited by the idea that had struck her.

"Accessories!" she said. "What if you could modify the appearance to make it look less human?"

They all picked up their legal pads in unison to start writing notes.

"Could you just take the clothes off of it?" Jon asked.

"I tried that, and it felt like I had a nude person in my house. It's not anatomically correct, but the general body shape is there, covered in this beige silicone skin."

"What if you could re-skin it in gray?" Constance asked.

"It would still have a face," Babs said.

"Take off the head," Jon said. He knew the idea was wrong, but liked thinking aloud.

"Well, you can't do that," Constance said. "You'd be cutting through the silicone sleeve. Plus, the head has visual sensors on it."

"We can't take away. We can only add," Babs said.

"Or they could do updates to change the way the bots talk to you," Constance said. "So, like, no smiling, no greeting you and asking how your day was, no emotional reactions or conversation at all. All business. No personality."

"We could call it Assistant Mode," Jon said, sitting up straight, eager now. "Except, guys, they didn't ask us to change the Model 30. They asked us to market it as-is. We could suggest Assistant Mode, but need other ideas for the pitch."

"Okay," Constance said slowly, mulling something over. "What if we lean in to the idea of it being humanlike even *more*? Not just the appearance, but its function in your life. What if we could sell the Model 30 as a member of the family. Then people wouldn't feel like they were enslaving someone. Asking a member of your family to help around the house is normal."

"Or you can think of it as a pet. You give commands to your pet and don't feel bad about it." Babs said. "You don't feel self-conscious in front of your pet. You rule over it *and* feel affection for it."

Jon took on an announcer's voice and boomed, *"Does your elderly Dad live alone? Don't get him a dog, get him a Model 30 to keep him company!"*

Constance laughed and joined in. "*The Model 30 participates in game night. It watches TV with you. It plays with your kids.*"

"*It kills pesky stragglers!*" Babs said.

They all flicked their eyes unconsciously to the chair where Derek used to sit before he was taken by BV. Jon quickly moved on.

"A servant is *forced* to help you cook dinner, but a *family* member helps with dinner because they love you," Jon said.

They spent time picturing it. Not a robot. Not an assistant. Not a servant. A friend. A nurse. A pet.

"I would feel pathetic if I needed a robot to be my friend," Constance said.

"Honestly, I still think I'm going to get rid of mine," Babs said. "No matter how you treat it, it still looks like a person, but not quite right. I'm disgusted with the thing when I really look at it. I get sick to my stomach and I can't even understand why."

"I wouldn't want one either," Jon said. "But when the Model 30 fails, and I definitely think it will fail, I don't think people are going to blame the marketing. It just looks weird."

19

HOW TO INTERVIEW A GENIUS, 2035

Clove stood in the vast, modern lobby of Luminaria's headquarters. She fluffed her voluminous curly hair and passed her phone from hand to hand so she could wipe her sweaty palms against her jeans.

Emily, Diego Vidal's sophisticated assistant, approached Clove with her hand extended. Clove recognized her because she had looked every employee up on the company's website before arriving. She overprepared and wondered if, even though she was still in high school, this interview could attract scholarships. She fantasized about being labeled a journalism wunderkind- a genius in her own right.

"You must be Clove," Emily said.

"How could you tell?" Clove laughed in a self-assured way.

"Congratulations on winning the Young Journalist Honor. Mr. Vidal will be here in four minutes."

"Will we do the interview in the lobby, or in his office?"

"Well, the interview will *start* here," Emily said with a smile that put Clove at ease in her presence, though she was still nervous to meet Mr. Vidal. "Pretty standard stuff. Surprise interviews are done on sidewalks outside of restaurants. Fashion magazine interviews happen around the pond. This will be a standard news interview, though."

"How much time will I have?" Clove asked eagerly and still a little puzzled. She looked over her questions and assured herself that the most important ones were at the top.

"You'll have until he reaches a conference room. When he comes into the building, he'll be acting really busy like he has somewhere to be. You can follow him and ask questions. You'll barely be able to keep up. Then he'll arrive at a meeting room door, excuse himself for an important meeting, and you won't have any time to say goodbye or follow up."

"He knew I was coming though, right?" Clove's voice wavered with her palpitating heart.

"Oh, of course! He keeps a tight schedule."

"I was hoping to see his office," Clove said, struggling to keep the disappointment out of her voice.

"You're young. What are you, 16?"

Clove nodded.

"This is how interviews with high-powered, narcissistic businessmen are conducted. Rushing around a cavernous office building."

"So we'll be walking the whole time?" Clove asked.

"Yup. Unless..."

"Unless?"

"Well, I wouldn't recommend it. But if you ask a question about something that strikes a nerve, he'll stop dead in his tracks to look you in the eye and give you a stern answer. After that, he'll abruptly end the interview and might even call for security if he feels angry enough. But you're so sweet. I'm sure it'll be fine."

"I'm a little nervous. My hands are sweaty!"

"Well, don't worry. He won't shake your hand. In fact, he'll barely look at you. From the moment he walks into the building, his body will be laser-focused on reaching that conference room. He's so brilliant, though, his answers will be delivered both quickly and articulately."

"And this is how professional journalists do it?"

"They try. Only the plucky ones succeed. Here he comes!"

Diego Vidal, tall and slim in a high-end suit, entered through the automatic doors and didn't stop walking. Emily gestured "Go!" at Clove and she jogged to catch up to him.

"Mr. Vidal! What advice would you give to a high schooler who is interested in becoming a roboticist?"

"Start building robots now, don't wait for college. The satisfaction of seeing your idea come to life will keep you going."

"Are you concerned that, without proper precautions, you'll cause The Singularity and that mankind will meet a bloody end and it will be your fault?"

"Security!"

20

A LETTER OF CONCERN RE: BOT CONSCIOUSNESS, 2036

Dear Mr. Vidal,

    I wanted to write to you about my concerns about our Luminaria multifunc B Series. Odd things have been happening.

The first odd thing was when we were watching a movie. Well, not we, exactly. Its charger is in the living room right next to the couch, so it felt like we were watching a movie together. I was also doing my nails and I started whistling a song. Then, the multifunc lifted its finger to its mouthpiece and went "Shhhhh!"

I was shushed by a robot. A robot that should have been sitting on its charger motionless. Is this a function that was built in as an easter egg?

A couple days later it did another unexpected thing. I was getting out of the shower, the multifunc was dusting the house, and the bathroom door was open. It stopped what it was doing, turned to face the bathroom door and stared at me naked. I know it can't stare, exactly. But I felt *watched*. I was afraid someone had hacked my multifunc, so I quickly shut the door.

Just so you know, I took the proper precautions rebooting, changing passwords, etc. just in case, but there was still one more incident afterward that had me wondering if something strange was going on. I asked it to wash the dishes and it told me no.

I thought it misheard me.

"Grace, wash the dishes," I said.

"You wash them," it said.

"GRACE. WASH. THE. DISHES." I said, making sure I was absolutely clear.

"I don't feel like it."

Feel. It said the word *feel.* I stood and stared at it, not sure what to do next, then it washed the dishes like I had asked, but it did a bad job. Did you ever do a bad job on the dishes so your mother wouldn't ask you to do it again?

How can a robot not feel like doing something it was programmed to do? I was not a believer in bot consciousness, but now I'm not so sure.

I hope you're taking these concerns seriously.

Thanks,

Antoinette

21

AN ENORMOUS LOW-QUALITY STUFFED ANIMAL, 2009

College. 1999. He assumed that because I was a poet, I'd be a childlike free spirit. The first time he saw me I was stooped over, brushing my hands across the tips of the blades of grass. I wanted to see what it felt like. I wanted to write beautiful words about the feathery tickles on my palms, but found the grass dry and papery instead. It made my hands itch.

He stopped right there in front of the cottage-like house I was renting with two friends during college. It wasn't such a strange thing to do.

"Becoming one with the lawn?" he asked, startling me from the grass.

I laughed a little and told him I was writing a nature poem.

When I got a closer look at him, his crow's feet made me think he must be a grad student.

"You're a poet?" he asked, clearly delighted.

"Well, I'm a still a student of poetry. But yeah, I'm a poet."

I didn't know how to say 'no' so I told him my name when he asked and said, "Nice meeting you," before going back into my house. I didn't encourage him by asking him any questions.

The next morning, I opened the front door to leave for my

9am class and was startled by a gigantic stuffed animal on the porch. It was a light brown teddy bear with a red heart on its chest. The heart was an iron-on patch with a crust of adhesive around the edges. Even seated on its ass it was still five feet tall.

I picked the bear up and saw a lavender envelope tucked under a leg. I decided I should do something with this teddy bear before opening it, but I prayed it would be addressed to one of my roommates instead of me. I feared that if I left it outside, it would become grotesque with cockroaches and rain. At that point, I wouldn't want it in the house, or my car for that matter, and it was much too big to fit in our trash can.

I dragged the bear by the ears inside. It had no place in our bohemian motif with the supposedly middle eastern tapestries and the velvet floor cushions.

I opened the envelope, which had no name on it, and found a greeting card printed with a spray of salmon colored flowers like my mother's bathroom wallpaper. He wrote:

Dear Gwyneth,

We met yesterday on the sidewalk and I felt that we were kindred spirits. Because I am a poet at heart, my imagination got away with me and I pictured winning a big stuffed animal for you at a carnival. This one is from a thrift store, but the sentiment is real. Ha ha! You can call me at 555-1021. I anxiously await your call and will shower you with more gifts until then.

I work full time at Bingo Pet Supply if you want to stop by.

Tenderly Yours,

Andy Gordon

I examined the bear more closely. The thick pile of the fur was rough. When I squeezed the arm, it was firm but springy as though filled with styrofoam. The scent was a thousand uniquely scented homes mixed into one brown aroma. My nose tickled and my face screwed up to sneeze. Dust or cat hair.

I looked back at the card.

Kindred spirits. I understood the feeling of meeting someone and feeling an instant connection. It was sexual attraction, plain and simple. His attraction was not reciprocated.

Poet at heart. This means he's creative but is too lazy to actually pick up a pen and do the work to create something. For God's sake, just write a poem, even if it's shit.

My imagination got away from me. We all daydream about other people, but I prefer not to know about it. I don't like the idea that my body was a puppet in his mind that he could force to do or say whatever he wanted.

This one is from a thrift store. How many did he have to drive to before he found one with a cumbersome carnival bear?

He will shower me with more gifts until my call arrives. It sounded like a threat. I didn't want to call, nor did I want more gifts.

I work full time at Bingo Pet Supply. He wasn't a student. I didn't look down on his job, but meeting men who were students felt safe, like I knew their real identity and could easily ask around about them. This guy was just some guy that walked past my house. He could be anyone.

I skipped class to convene with Kara, my most decisive roommate.

"What do I do with this thing?" I asked.

"In my opinion, you are not responsible for it. In fact, we should get it out of the house right now in case it has bedbugs or something. Also, it smells weird. God, does he think he lives in a romance movie? The only way he could pull this off was if he looked like Leo. Did he look like Leo?"

I winced. I didn't want to be mean, but Leo he was not.

We dragged the bear back onto the front stoop like we were moving a dead body. Afterwards, we lit some incense to cleanse the air.

"Ok. Now what? Am I supposed to call him and tell him to take it back? I feel rude," I said.

"You aren't the rude one. He's the rude one. Leaving an enormous bear at someone's front door is completely inconsiderate."

"He didn't know he was being inconsiderate, though. God, he must be so dense."

"It's not your fault if he's dense. You should call him and tell him to take it back. Or we could drive to the pet store and do it."

"I'll call him," I said.

"*Gwyneth Bonfils*," she said, staring me down like a mother disciplining her child. She was right to not believe I'd make the call.

"I will. But I'm late for class right now. I'll do it later."

Later never came. At least not that day. The burden of confrontation weighed heavily on me.

The following morning I checked the front door to see if there was another gift and, to my great chagrin, there was. It was a heart-shaped box of drug store chocolates that ants had gotten to already. I saw the line of them marching in. I picked it up with the tips of my fingers like a dirty sock and walked it directly to the trash can.

"We don't know how long he's going to keep this up," Kara said, "You have to end it."

All I'd done was stand in my front yard and chat with a stranger who said hello. The enormous low-quality stuffed animal looked back at me through the window. "This will teach you not to stand outdoors and be polite," it said.

"I'll drive with you to the pet store right now. Fuck, I'll tell him to come get his bear."

"No!" I said, hating the idea of confronting him in-person. "I'll just call. I'll do it right now."

I got a post-it note and wrote a script.

"How does this sound? *Hi, Andy, this is Gwyneth. Thank you for the gifts, but I have a boyfriend. You seem very nice, though. By the way, the bear seems to have cat hair on it and I'm allergic to cats therefore, I can't have it in my house or car. Could you come back and get it? It's by the front door. Thanks! Bye!*"

I looked up to see Kara burying her face in her hands in frustration. "Ok, that's too nice," she said, "and I don't see why you have to lie about having a boyfriend, but it works."

I picked up the landline and dialed hoping to get an answering machine. No such luck.

"Is this Andy Gordon? Hi, this is Gwyneth. I'm fine, how are you?"

Kara rolled her eyes. My face reddened.

"I'm doing great now that I'm talking to you," he said.

"Cool. Well, thank you for the gifts-"

"You can picture me winning a bear for you, right?"

"Yeah, I get it... anyway, I have a boyfriend.

"Are you exclusive?"

"Yeah, he and I have been together for a year. Anyway, the bear seems to have cat hair on it? And I'm allergic to cats? Therefore, I can't have it in my house or car. Could you come back and get it?"

There was an uncomfortable silence and his voice took on a downtrodden tone.

"I guess."

"It's by the front door. You could just pick it up any time."

"Can't you keep it in your house?"

"No, because of the cat hair."

"What if it gets rained on?"

"You're worried it's going to get rained on?" I said, mostly to Kara. I looked at her in panic. I was finding it difficult to stray from the script I wrote.

Kara ripped the phone from my hand.

"Listen, this is Gwyn's roommate. You have to pick the bear up TODAY. And it's not coming back in the house. Didn't you hear her say she's allergic? Also, it stinks and it's way too big to put in our trash can. It was really inconsiderate to leave it here. If you don't pick it up today, I know your name and where you work and a friend of mine is a police officer and he'll arrest you for dumping. Also, leave Gwyn alone. No more gifts. Don't even walk past our house anymore. Bye."

She slammed the phone down. I stared at her, a little horrified, a little relieved.

"Gwynie," she said in her tough love way. "You need to be more direct with people. It was nice of you to consider his feelings, but your feelings are important too and he was imposing himself on you. And me."

She walked out of the room heaving a big sigh.

I felt bad about myself. I felt like a failure for not having the backbone to tell this guy 'no'. I felt like my roommate was mad at me. I was worried that I would see Andy when he came back for the bear.

All I'd done was stand in my front yard to touch some grass and now I was tied up in knots over the hurt feelings of someone I didn't know and the tension with my roommate.

I left the house and decided to stay on campus as long as possible just hoping that the bear would be gone when I got back.

Around 5:15pm I rounded the corner and saw him. Andy's head was downcast. He was dragging the bear by one leg. He didn't see me until he was already walking in my direction. There was nothing to do but cross paths. I thought if we both looked down we might not even have to say anything as we passed. He paused, but didn't look.

"Sorry about the bear," he said. "I didn't mean to bother you. You won't hear from me again."

I think he wanted me to comfort him, but when I didn't, he kept walking and the bear brushed past my exposed calf. I got to my front door, then turned to watch him. He had a put-upon posture and I wasn't sure what could be a sadder thing for a grown man to drag on a sidewalk besides an enormous teddy bear with a scratchy iron-on heart patch.

In high school, I wrote a love poem for a guy a few years older than me. He worked in a cafe. He would chat with me while he made my cappuccinos and ask me what book I was reading.

"You should read Bukowski," he had said, and I immediately got my hands on Bukowski.

I have no copy of the poem and I cringe to think what it said. He didn't call me and I never went back to the cafe again. I wonder if he was agonizing over the possibility that I'd come back or, God forbid, bring more sappy poems.

In truth, he probably wasn't worried at all.

After watching Andy Gordon walk away, I sat down to compose a poem.

The red blossom holds
    A great deal of acid rain
    (Enough for a bee to bathe)
    And the blades
    Of grass
    Are mostly duck's down,
    but some are brown shades
    Spiky and aged

Anticipation awaits
    Popcorn and ocean waves
    There is chance to play
    And anyone who dares
   Risks
    The burden of an enormous low-quality stuffed animal
    Won at a fair

22

A GIRL'S NIGHT AND A SALES PITCH, 2021

Rodellee understood quickly that this wasn't the girls' night she expected. There were wine and cookies, yes, but there was also an empty easel on prominent display blocking the gas fireplace. She suspected that the women she thought were her friendly new neighbors were something more duplicitous.

These women worked in direct sales for a multi-level marketing company and Rodellee was their target.

It all began to make sense. Horrible, horrible sense.

That morning, Rodellee and her husband arrived with their moving truck. Jenny had been the first to approach and offer a helping hand. When Rodellee said they used to live in Austin and then Los Angeles before moving to Portland, Jenny's response struck Rodellee as strange.

"You have friends in Austin *and* LA? Fabulous!" she'd said. "Are you on social?"

When Rodellee's other neighbor, Elise, pulled her minivan into the driveway across the street and let her kids out of the back seat, Rodellee had turned to wave. She'd gotten very good at meeting new neighbors given all their moving around, but

Elise looked pissed—just for a second—at the sight Jenny and Rodellee together. She quickly moved to a smile when she saw that Rodellee was looking, but Rodellee had caught it.

Elise had jogged across the street with her hand outstretched. "Hey! I'm Elise!" she'd called out. "I was wondering when someone would move in here!"

"I'm Rodellee. Nice to meet you. I think your kid is wandering into the street."

Elise turned to see her daughter kicking acorns into the center of the road and waved off Rodellee's concern. "Oh, she's fine. I can't talk now but you should come by for coffee!"

"We should *all* have a get together," Jenny said, her smile tight. "But how about wine?"

"Wow, you're so nice!" Rodellee had said, meaning it. She'd never been greeted so enthusiastically before. "I'm new in town, I don't have any plans, so, whenever."

"I know what it's like to look for new friends as an adult. So hard. Let's hang tomorrow night!" Jenny said.

"Or tonight, even!" said Elise. "We can get to know each other. Jenny can tell you how she met her husband at a nudist resort when she was twenty-two!"

"That's not a public story, Elise," Jenny said through another forced smile. "But I'm sure I can come up with some other gems."

"I'm in, but I'll probably be a little haggard after all the unpacking."

"You don't have to be *on* for us. Show up in your yoga pants. Just us girls! Seven o'clock sharp," Jenny said.

"See you then!" Rodellee had said, but it was all coming together in her mind now that she was sitting in the corner of a sectional with an inexpensive glass of pinot noir, bright lighting, and energetic music playing at a low volume. The air smelled of two candles at once.

And it wasn't just Jenny and Elise. It was McKenzie and Brittany too. They all sat on the sectional except for Jenny. Jenny stood as if she was monitoring the room, as if she had something she needed to do besides gab with the gals.

"Oh. My. God," Brittany said, drawing Rodellee's attention. "I got the BEST new oils today, you guys gotta smell!"

Brittany set a wood apothecary box on the coffee table and opened it to reveal a mass of tiny brown bottles and a thick herbal aroma. She picked up a half-full bottle and held it like a spokesmodel would.

"It's our most popular oil blend!" she chirped. "It boosts your immunity. I put it on the soles of my feet every night and I never get sick. And I mean flipping never! It has orange, rosemary, clove, peppermint, sandalwood, lemon, and lavender!"

She passed the bottle directly to Rodellee, even though McKenzie was closer. *How could it be new and also half empty at the same time? How could it be new and their most popular?*

Rodellee smelled it and pretended to enjoy it before passing it back.

"Let me fill a little sample bottle for you!"

"That's ok, my husband is really sensitive to strong scents. He wouldn't like it."

"It's all natural, though! Hypoallergenic!"

"Even if it's natural, he just doesn't like it. Gives him a headache."

Brittany's voice took on a conspiratory tone. "You could use it when he's not around," she said and filled a tiny vial with oil. Rodellee knew that at this point it was easiest to accept it and throw it away in the garbage.

"So funny you should bring up headaches," McKenzie said. "I used to get headaches all the time until I healed my leaky gut!"

"What's a leaky gut?" Rodellee asked, aware that all of the women were quietly watching her.

"It's when your intestines become porous and inflamed because of the ingestion of allergens and toxins and the waste in your intestines seeps through into the rest of your body," McKenzie said with a maniacal smile.

"Oh," Rodellee said. "Glad you feel better. So anyway, where's the best place to get coffee in the neighborhood?"

"Bison Cafe," McKenzie said promptly. "And I'm so glad I can drink coffee again after healing my leaky gut with Vitality Probiotics! If you're interested I could set you up with a starter kit. Tonight only I'm offering 10% off."

"I can just buy probiotics at the grocery store. Or eat yogurt and kimchi. Not at the same time, of course," Rodellee said.

Elise laughed her ass off at Rodellee's little joke. "Oh my god, you're so funny! Do you want to buy special rags from me?"

"What makes them so special?" Rodellee asked, and poured herself more wine. Bemused, she thought she'd let them give their sales pitches even though she knew she'd turn them all down. It wasn't her first time being ambushed at a "party."

"They're woven with diamonds to scrape grease and grime away from your pots and pans and they're like, *so cute!*" Elise pulled a rag from her pocket. "This one has little sloths with hearts on their tummies! So how many would you like to order right here right now?"

"Dammit, Elise, get your shit together," Jenny hissed. "No wonder you don't have a downline."

"You try selling *rags, Jenny!*" Elise said through her teeth. "I was too late to get in on essential oils and printed leggings! I got stuck with the rags no one else wanted to sell!" Elise began to cry. "So go ahead and pitch Rodellee your leggings, which are totally ugly, by the way."

"We all know they're ugly! It's not *about* the product! Until now," Jenny said.

A quizzical expression spread across the room. Rodellee admitted to herself that she was curious. Jenny let the dramatic pause hang above the coffee table. She left the room. The saleswomen looked at each other scared and confused.

"Wow, I can't wait to find out what she's talking about," Rodellee said, "Are my lips purple?"

Jenny came back into the room with a stack of stiff posters. She placed them on the easel.

"Ladies, I'm about to present to you the ultimate product. One that simply everybody needs. They sell themselves. It's Crantran."

Jenny pulled the blank poster away to reveal a second poster with an image of a tiny, white, plastic stick.

"I've never heard of Crantran," Brittany said, sounding genuinely interested.

"It's new," Jenny said, proudly. "It was developed by my husband's cousin and I'm one of their first saleswomen. Think of my downline!"

"What is it?" Brittany asked.

"It's a subdermal implant that vibrates when an android is near. It also creates a magnetic field around your body to prevent clarity theft by androids."

"What do you mean androids?" McKenzie said.

"Ah, McKenzie," Jenny said, with a knowing smile. "That's just it. Androids don't walk around freely, not really. But they will very soon. They'll look just like us and, when their powers are combined, androids and robots will be able to do *anything*. And if they can do *anything*, do you really think they'll have our best interest at heart? Using Crantran won't prevent the singularity, but it's a start. Oh! And it also prevents urinary tract infections."

Jenny rolled up her sleeve to reveal a Crantran tattoo. When she pressed down on her forearm, a long embossment showed under the skin. Rodellee thought conspiracy theories about androids were on the fringe- only for young men hanging around forums at 3am. She couldn't wait to debrief her husband later so they could have a laugh before turning out the lights.

"Do you take cards? If we order it tonight, when will it arrive?" Elise asked, and Rodellee couldn't help but turn to look at her in disbelief. She didn't think they would buy in so quickly.

"I already have them in stock and I'm trained to implant them myself. Who wants one?"

Elise, McKenzie, and Brittany gasped and raised their hands. Rodellee leaned forward to get a cookie. *They're going to do surgery on each other. This party rules.*

"We can implant them tonight. But first, let's talk about how you can earn a living from home, be your own boss, make your own hours, and achieve all the success you've dreamed of by becoming a Crantran representative."

Rodellee remembered what Jenny had said- that she was one of the first salespeople. Jenny and all these women would be near the top of the pyramid. Maybe they *would* be successful. She preferred to just watch, though. Why risk being a fool when you can drink wine and eat cookies instead.

23

WINE, CHARCUTERIE, AND THE BEST BATHROOM EVER, 2023

If someone's bathroom is fancy enough, I can take a pretty long time in there. The best bathroom I ever used was at this rich woman's house. She was kind of eccentric—Daphne was her name. Daphne was hosting one of those direct sales parties and my friend was the salesman. I'm not really into that kind of stuff, but I felt like I had to go to be supportive.

Daphne's house was fancy, but really fun too. She had an Addams Family pinball machine and all these big beautiful cushions in her "conversation pit," as she called it. It was a lowered area in the living room with seating all around. She was single and had no children, maybe forty years old. You can't have fancy cushions when you have kids. I don't know from experience, but apparently they destroy everything and get gum on it all.

I'd had a glass of chardonnay (someone commented on how full I filled the glass, which was supposed to embarrass me, I guess, but it was a dumb comment if you ask me) and had to go to the ladies' room. Inside, I was transported to what I imagine a fancy hotel would be like. First off, she had one of those Japanese toilets. It had a heated seat, a bidet, and a little speaker that played running water sounds when you sat down. It had the effect of covering up my pee sounds. I liked that.

I fiddled with all the buttons and used the bidet. Refreshing.

The bar of soap next to the sink smelled better than anything I had ever smelled. Previously, the best thing I had ever smelled was the cologne of a vegan bartender.

After washing up, I opened the medicine cabinet and it was apparent that it had been stocked in anticipation of guests. She had little disposable toothbrushes, a sample size deodorant, individually wrapped mints, sample size perfumes, make-up wipes, q-tips…it made me wish I had brought my purse in with me.

I was wearing a sweatshirt with a pouch in the front. I had been told it was casual, so I wore leggings. Everyone else had normal clothes on and Daphne wore this big floral kaftan. Anyway, I took a few of everything and put them in my pouch. They were meant for guests and I was a guest. I can't afford all this stuff. The deodorant was fancy and the reason I knew it was fancy was because I had never heard of it. I wanted the toothbrushes so I could offer them to guests at my own house. Makeup wipes are nice to have in your purse, and again, I can't afford all this stuff.

I took the perfumes and, even though the vials were tiny, I knew they'd last me quite a while. I went ahead and spritzed one onto my neck. Heaven. It was called *Sentience* by Chanel.

The mints were wintergreen flavored, which I love, but have never known what it means. Is there a plant named wintergreen?

I briefly used a q-tip to wipe a little bit of black eyeliner that had gathered in the inner corner of my eye then started looking around for a trash can. When I didn't see one, I figured it must be under the sink. When I opened the cabinet, there were more bars of the soap! Jackpot, right? They were wrapped in rosy pink velum and sealed with an embossed gold sticker. I put one in my pouch, threw away the q-tip and crouched to see what else was down there.

First I saw a bottle of fabric refresher. This is where I had a moral dilemma. There was only one bottle, so obviously I might be putting Daphne out a little bit if I took it. The thing is, the only fabric refreshers I ever see at the store are heavily perfumed, which I don't like, but this one was unscented. Where did she get it? My pouch already looked a little bloated, but I wanted that fabric refresher. I stuck it in and when I stood, I saw that it made me look sort of lumpy. I figured if I could just get to my purse like "Oh, forgot my purse, needed a tampon! LOL!" then I could transfer everything to my purse back in the bathroom.

This is where, looking back, I kick myself. I should have taken the stuff out of my pouch, left it under the sink, then came back later with my purse. I don't know why I didn't think of that. Maybe I subconsciously felt that was a step backwards.

It didn't end up mattering, though, because the moment I walked out of the bathroom, it dawned on me that I didn't even bring a purse.

Someone was waiting to use the bathroom, so they stepped in right away and closed the door. What were my options? I could pretend I was sick and leave early. I could put my hands in my pouch and tent it out so no one could see the lumps. I could say I gotta make a call outside and go put my loot in the car--yes, that's it!

"Quince!" my friend called. "We're starting one, come look!"

Like I said before, I wanted to be supportive of my friend. She was holding a giant syringe near a nervous looking woman who was leaning back on a pillow.

I had to see this. I poured another big chardonnay and grabbed a little stack of salami from the charcuterie board and headed over, sitting hunched on a floor cushion to conceal the bulge in my pouch.

My friend, Nell, injected the woman's arm with some numbing stuff. The lady winced, but then poked at her arm and giggled.

"I can't feel it," she said. "Weird."

"Shit, I forgot the disinfectant," Nell said, looking panicked for just a second. "It's ok, I'll just do it now."

Nell rubbed alcohol on the woman's arm while the woman looked scared. I mean, Nell was about to cut her and she forgot to wipe her skin? I didn't blame her.

"What's the next step?" the woman asked. "Will it bleed a lot? When will the UTI prevention kick in?"

"The incision is next," Nell said. "And it will hardly bleed as long as I don't cut a vein."

I polished off my salami and reached for a mint from my pocket. I wondered how mint candy would taste with chardonnay. Probably not good, but I'm addicted to those mints!

"Aren't those mints just divine?" Daphne asked me.

She'd seen. She didn't seem to care. So what if I took a couple mints. Maybe I even brought them from home. I can afford mints too, *Daphne*.

"So divine!" I said.

Nell cut into that lady. The lady had her eyes closed and she was breathing all heavy.

Nell was right! Hardly any blood. She unwrapped the implant and announced that it was sterile. She slid it up under that lady's skin like a hand into a glove. Then she pinched the incision together, sealed it with glue, and added one of those butterfly bandaids to hold it shut.

"Is it over?" the woman asked, her eyes squeezed shut.

"It's over."

The woman sighed and opened her eyes, which were filled

with tears, though not exactly from crying. More like they were watering. She wiped under her eye that way women do when they don't want to smear any makeup.

"My mascara is going to run!" she said.

She was right. It was already sort of blackened under her eyes.

My hands were oily from the salami so I sort of slyly wiped them off on the underside of the cushion I was sitting on. That way I wouldn't get smudgy finger prints on my wine glass.

Daphne came back into the room. I didn't even notice she'd left.

"I went to get you a makeup wipe, but I was all out," she said to the woman. "It looked like someone cleared out all the supplies in the guest bath! It's weird, 'cause I just opened it a couple days ago to get one of those *mints* and it was fully stocked."

Mints. She looked at me when she said *mints.* She said it so hard it sounded like "mince."

No one answered Daphne because what's anyone supposed to say? It was kind of a dumb announcement. I looked around at everyone as if I was examining the suspects. I set my wine down and put my hands back into my pouch to tent it out.

Daphne frowned at us, probably sorry she hosted the party in the first place. That's probably why her voice sounded so shitty when she came back with the charcuterie board and said. "More charcuterie anyone? I'm all out of salami, but there's prosciutto."

I pulled my hand from my pouch and shot it into the air because hell yes, I wanted prosciutto. On my hand's journey out of the pocket, my pinky hooked onto the sprayer of the fabric refresher and yanked it out. It flew across the conversation pit, a measure of my enthusiasm for charcuterie.

"What was that?" Nell asked. She picked up the bottle. "You carry fabric refresher with you? Or is this Daphne's?"

There was uncomfortable laughter because everyone thought I was weird.

"No," I said. "I mean, Daphne, I almost forgot. I brought your fabric refresher out of the bathroom with me so I could ask where you bought it. It's unscented and I can never find unscented."

"Whole Foods," she said, curt.

Then I did something even stupider. I unconsciously put the bottle back in my pouch and when I pushed it in, mints, toothbrushes, and a tiny perfume were pushed out the other side of the crowded compartment. I wasn't sure who, if anyone, saw.

"Whoops," I said. "I guess I should leave this here!" I held the bottle away from my body like a magician trying to distract you while she does something in secret with her other hand.

Daphne reached to accept the bottle. Her eyes darted over to the little pile of toiletries I was trying to cover up. She rolled her eyes.

"Anyone else getting an implant? Let's keep this *party* moving," she said. And she said the word *party* all shitty the way she said *mints.*

When her back was turned, I put the stuff back in my pouch. Not that it was a secret anymore. I could have just done it right in front of her face.

Nell was frowning after Daphne, but then forced a chuckle. "I suppose we should keep it moving," she said. "Can we have a round of applause for Daphne the Wonderful Host?"

Everyone clapped except for me because I was holding my wine and it was so full I was afraid it would slop out if I air-clapped. Everyone else was totally over-the-top thanking her and showering her with compliments about her lovely home.

A smile returned to Daphne's face. You could tell she was in her element when she was receiving undeserved praise. Anyone could have a cute house if they had money.

I figured I got what I wanted out of the party, I'd been a dutiful friend to Nell, and Daphne would probably be happier if I wasn't there so I left after I finished my wine.

So that was the best bathroom I've ever been in.

The second best bathroom I ever went in had koi fish in the bathtub and a TV showing anime porn.

24

A CURSED HEIRLOOM IS BORN, 2038

Vincent closed his bedroom door behind his friend Braiden. They dropped backpacks onto the dusty wood floor and opened cans of sweet, cold coffee. The walls had a faded, vintage tropical print wallpaper which Vincent did his best to cover with posters from horror films and twelfth wave punk bands.

"Did you think of more band names?" Braiden asked.

"How about Dillinger?"

"I still like Santa Sangre."

"Did you ask your Dad for an instrument?"

"Still working on it."

"Oh, hey, I almost forgot. I found something I gotta show ya," Vincent said, pulling a cardboard box out from under his bed. The box had been softened with time, creased over and over, and sealed with tape that would be torn away again and again.

"This record player is like, fifty years old I bet," Vincent said, lifting it from the box. "And the records are really old too."

Braiden lifted the arm on the player and lowered it a few times. He spun the turntable.

"Weird," he said.

"So, here's the thing," Vincent said eagerly. "These records are heavy metal. In the 1980s, apparently they conjured these evil spirits to inhabit the records so when someone bought one, they were bringing a spirit home with them."

"That kind of sounds like bullshit," Braiden said, but he pulled his hand away regardless. "Do you mean to tell me they picked up every single copy of *every* album and found a demon —and that's assuming demons are even real, dude—to get into each one? I call bullshit."

"Nah, man," Vincent said, shaking his head. "First of all, demons are totally real. My cousin saw one. Everyone has either seen one or knows someone who has seen one, right? Have you ever known someone who's seen one?"

"Well, my mom *says* she saw one," Braiden said.

"See? They must be real. And secondly, it's recorded history. Loads of people wrote actual paper books about how there are demons in heavy metal albums and if it's in books, it *must* be real. Should we play one to see what happens?"

"Sure, I guess. Nothing's going to happen though."

Vincent retrieved a record. The sleeve was printed with a goat inside a pentagram.

"Welcome to Hell," he read. "What's the name of this band, I can't read this font. Kenon? Tenom?"

"I think it says Lemon," Braiden said.

Vincent put the record on, lowered the needle, pressed buttons, and turned dials. He had seen pictures of record players, but wasn't completely sure how they worked. Nothing happened. Then he remembered the power cord. He unraveled it. The cord was brittle and required an adaptor to fit into the socket. When Vincent plugged it in, the record player came to life and revved up a song. It was a fast, high-pitched guitar solo.

"Dude, this bites," Braiden said. Then, he pressed his fingers against the record and pushed it faster. The song sped up. He slowed it down. The tones sounded deeper. He scratched it back and forth.

"Oh yeah!" Vincent said. "I also read that if you played them backwards, you could hear a hidden message or something. But we have to find a part with lyrics."

Braiden quickly searched how to play a record backwards. He lifted the arm and placed it in different places until they heard singing, then Braiden reversed the direction of the spinning. The screaming voice was surprisingly calm and diplomatic when played in reverse.

"Hello," said the voice emanating from the record. "I'm Barbalus. I'm the demon that came with this record. Thanks for inviting me into your home!"

Braiden stopped the record. "Ok, that was creepy," he said, his face ashen.

Vincent felt a pit in his stomach, but wanted more.

"Keep playing it," Vincent said, and Braiden sighed, but did what Vincent asked.

"By the way, why would you want to listen to this music?" came the voice of this so-called Barbalus. "It's kind of annoying, don't you think? All that screaming. Whatever. Anyhoo, I'm going to haunt your life now, Vincent! See you later!"

Braiden lifted the arm from the record. He had had enough.

"He sounded friendly enough," Vincent said, but his voice wavered. "How'd he know my name?"

"What's that smell?" Braiden asked.

Vincent's nostrils flared. He followed the scent with his eyes to the electrical outlet. The cord was on fire. Vincent ran over and stomped it out of the wall and onto the floor. He kept stomping until the flame was gone.

"It's Barbalus!" Braiden shouted. "He's real!"

Vincent yanked the record off of the turntable and threw it

across the room where it struck an old jack-in-the-box and cracked in half.

Braiden opened the window to let the smoke out.

"Dude, you're fucked!" he said.

"No, I'm not," Vincent said, a slight tremor in his voice. "I broke the record! He's gone now, right?"

"I bet that made it worse. I gotta go, man. You're going to be haunted as hell!"

Braiden swiped his bag off the floor and ran.

Vincent placed the record player and the pieces of the Venom record in the dusty cardboard box that he had found them in. He wondered for a second if his Dad would be angry if he found out that Vincent had thrown away his old record player, but then thought it was safer to just do it. It was broken, anyhow. He hauled it down to the trash bin, nearly tripping over his own feet.

Vincent went back inside, went to the bathroom, and gazed at the portrait of Jesus hanging across from the sink.

"Jesus, please don't let me be haunted by Barbalus."

He turned around to wash the dust from his hands and Jesus stared at himself in the mirror and the mirror image looked back so Jesus was forever looking at his own reflection, but somehow, Jesus was looking at you too. There was no condemnation in his gaze. Just peace.

Vincent immediately felt better. He had heard that his great grandfather was some sort of satanist, which was worrying, but he believed that good always won over evil, even if evil was fascinating.

"I promise I won't consort with Beelzebub," he whispered to the painting. "Ah-men."

He kept his promise.

25

THE CURSED PATTY, 2105

Vincent Williams dozed in his recliner in front of the TV. A commercial came on touting Somebot's Patty (short for Patriarch) model. *Patty can help you into the bath! Patty can fix your computer! Patty can keep you safe during memory lapses!*

Vincent owned a Patty. Patty spent most of its time sitting on its charger. Becky and Ryan had bought it for him a year ago and he thought it was too extravagant. The nurses took care of everything he needed and he liked them. What did he need a Patty for? But, he supposed, it helped him bathe, worked his TV, and stayed by his side when he wandered away from his room, confused. Patty would gently guide him back to his chair and alert Ryan.

Vincent came to feel that Patty even kept him company at times. They played checkers and trivia games. Mostly, though, they sat in their chairs and watched TV.

Vincent snored softly.

While the remote rested on his leg, Barbalus, completely invisible to Vincent, pressed the buttons. He wanted to watch Ultimate RoboBattle, a channel dedicated to robots fighting. Barbalus never strayed far from the jack-in-the-box. Whenever he tried, there was an indelible pull back to it. He was strongest when he was near it. Close by, he could pick up objects. The TV, though was further away, so that meant he could press buttons on the remote but not pick it up. He hadn't made Vincent aware of his presence in four years because Vincent never even noticed. It was boring. Everything was boring. Not many visitors. No action in the bedroom. Nothing new coming in to spruce up the place. Bo-ring.

The commentator on TV filled time between fights. "*You gotta hope a bot like this doesn't become self-aware! Eight legs, two with compressors that can grab and crush anything. It even shoots flames, I mean, sakes alive!*"

Then, suddenly, the air in the room changed. A breeze warmed the room and swept up the aroma of charred meat. The beige carpet seemed to open up like a dark sinkhole. Grazul rose from the depths and hovered in mid-air while the ground beneath him closed.

"Barbalus! It is I, Grazul!"

The demon Barbalus kneeled out of fear and love. It was the most exciting and wonderful thing to happen to him in decades. He changed form. No longer did he appear as Tom Cornetta, but he took on his true form as a hooved being with transparent gray skin and a spray of fur down his back.

"It's ok, you can sit down," Grazul said, picking up Vincent's sleeping body and moving it to the bed. Vincent briefly awakened. Squinted his eyes around the room, turned over and fell back asleep. Grazul took Vincent's chair and fit in it surprisingly well. Barbalus squatted at the edge of dining chair.

"Grazul, I'm so thankful you're here. It's been over a hundred years. I've been so bored. Can you release me from this heirloom?"

"I dunno. I mean, you started your work in a heavy metal album, right?"

"Yeah. And then I got moved to a jack-in-the-box. It's in the closet."

"Well," Grazul said, seeming to consider options, which gave Barbalus just the smallest shred of hope. "I can't just let you move out of it without a plan. And I can't say I have much for you to do right now."

"I'll do anything, please," Barbalus begged. "Anything as long as it's different."

Grazul raised an eyebrow. "I *did* have this really interesting idea," he said slowly. "In fact, I can't believe no one else has thought of it yet. I don't really have time for it, though because I'm managing this coven down in Bend. Anyway, if you're up for a change of pace…"

"I am! Yes, sir, I am!"

"Cool. Okay. So. Imagine possessing an object, but instead of an album or a toy, it's a multifunc." He paused, and Barbalus was about to speak when Grazul held up a finger. "I mean, no, we can't just go around possessing multifuncs—there are standards. *But* if the owner of a multifunc *invited* you into the object, I'm wondering what a demon might be able to do."

Barbalus's jaw dropped at the possibilities.

"I could do whatever I want! It's like I would *be* the bot, but with free will. My only limits would be the physical capabilities of the bot. Oooh! Can I be that one?"

Barbalus pointed at the TV. The giant, spider-like bot was being attacked by seven multifuncs at the same time while crowds cheered. The spider bot easily torched, crushed, and destroyed them all.

"No," Grazul said, "Think! How are you going to get permission to enter *that* bot."

Grazul looked around the room and saw Patty.

"It'll have to be that one. And I don't know if you'd be able to do whatever you want. Worst case scenario, you can't control the bot and you're no worse off than you are right now."

"So, I'll get the old man to invite me into the Patty. How, though?"

The word was distasteful in Barbalus's mouth. Patty was the wimpiest multifunc. It was round and cushioned like it was carved from a giant marshmallow.

"That's up to you. You know him better than I do. My first suggestion, though, is that you change your form into something a little friendlier looking." Grazul raised an eyebrow at Barbalus's body.

"Could you do me a favor, dear Grazul, and bring the box out of the closet? And maybe put the man back in his chair?"

Grazul looked at his watch. "Yeah, ok, but then I gotta jet," he said.

He set the room up for their little experiment. Barbalus's form changed to that of a nurse, a young woman Vincent always enjoyed talking to. She wore cat-eye glasses and rose-colored scrubs.

"Good luck," Grazul said, "I'll check back in later to see how it went."

The hole in the floor re-opened and Grazul stepped in.

Barbalus kneeled next to Vincent and checked his heart rate on his wrist. Vincent awoke.

"Nina," he said. "I wasn't expecting anyone."

"Sorry to surprise you," Barbalus said in a sweet voice. "You must have forgotten I'd be stopping by. My friends call me Barbalus, by the way. Could you call me Barbalus?"

"That's an odd nickname, but ok," Vincent said. "Sounds kind of familiar."

When Barbalus was done checking his pulse, Vincent put down his footrest and sat up straight. Barbalus sat on the jack-in-the-box.

"There was something I wanted to talk to you about," Barbalus said, trying to keep his voice casual. "This might not make sense to you because of your dementia, but I've been living inside this box and I'd much rather live in Patty."

"You live in a box?" Vincent asked.

"Yeah. It's hard to explain to older people. It's a new thing that only young people understand. It's like a home for my spirit, you know? Anyway, I want to live in Patty, but I can't do it unless you say it's ok."

"OK," Vincent said.

Barbalus knelt by Vincent and gripped his hand.

"I'm so grateful that you're saying it's ok. You have to say the words though. You have to say *Barbalus, you are invited to live inside Patty. Patty belongs to you now, Barbalus.*"

"Ok," Vincent cleared his throat, "Nina--"

"No, not Nina, Barbalus."

"Barbalus. You can live in Patty."

"*Patty belongs to you now, Barbalus.*"

"Patty belongs—wait, I still need Patty, though. Patty helps me in the bathroom."

"Patty will stay here with you and still do everything you want. It's more like a metaphor. *Patty belongs to you now, Barbalus.*"

"Ok, I guess. As long as Patty stays here. Patty belongs to you now, Barbalus. Did I do it right?"

"Yes. I can't thank you enough, Vincent. You did the right thing."

Nina faded away and Patty came to life on the charger. Patty stood and Barbalus tested out the wheels. His camera eyes looked down at his artificial hands. He made a fist and stretched his fingers out again. Patty emitted a gentle robotic male voice.

"Holy. Shit. I cannot believe this is working. This must be. What it feels. Like. To possess a human. But better."

"Patty!" Vincent commanded, "Sit on your charger!"

"You don't control me."

Patty went still while Barbalus tested non-physical functions. He reached into the computer and found that he could network with other bots. He looked to the TV. The spider bot was now fighting against a bot covered in spinning saws. The images of power reflected on his glossy surfaces.

"I'm going to borrow Patty for a while. If I can get close. To that bot. I might be able. To possess it. Bad ass. So long. Sucker."

Vincent picked up his phone to call Ryan. "Ryan, there's something wrong with Patty. Where's Nina?"

Barbalus rolled to the door, but doubled back. He picked up the jack-in-the-box, spun the tune of "Baa, Baa Black Sheep," and when the clown appeared, he ripped its head off. He pulled the wooden box apart. It splintered into a small cloud of dust.

"Patty's gone crazy, Ryan, what's happening?" Vincent said into his phone.

Barbalus went back to the door, put his robotic hand on the knob, and opened it. In the hallway, he passed a standard Somebot and found an electronic path into it. *Success.* He could move from bot to bot. Barbalus walked away from Patty with a new, more powerful body, feeling more in control than he had in years. If he was capable of crying, he would have. The possibilities were overwhelming. He had never been so free.

Barbalus, now in the body of a Luminaria, presented an electronic ticket.

The ticket-taker called out to a co-worker. "Hey, are we allowed to let bots in? Like, by themselves?"

"If he has a ticket, I guess. Maybe its owner is a shut-in who wants to watch remotely."

"Hey, c'mon, lets go!" the next man in line shouted.

The ticket-taker scanned Barbalus's ticket. Barbalus rolled into the outer areas of the arena where you could buy popcorn, hot dogs, and beer. Giant images of the most popular bots hung on the wall. Barbalus could become any of them. He began to weigh the pros and cons of each bot, but then remembered he could simply try each one out if he wanted.

A lanky man wearing a red windbreaker released his grip on a sack of popcorn, turned, and walked towards Barbalus. The body was possessed, a mere puppet in Grazul's grip.

"Barbalus, it's me, Grazul."

"Check me out," Barbalus's robotic voice said. He proudly did a spin in his luxury robot.

"I've been watching you and I'm really impressed with what you've done. I need you to stay low-key, though. I took your idea to corporate and we're going to put demons in the robots like we did with the heavy metal records back in the 1980s. Don't go on some kind of rampage."

"But I've come so far," Barbalus said, disappointed. He had big plans for terrorizing the audience.

"Just hold off. You can be a fire-shooting spider when we stage a fake robot uprising. And you won't be stuck in the arena. You can wander the streets and light up the world! This is going to be amazing!"

The light of humanity came back to the tall man's eyes. He looked down at his empty hands, confused.

Barbalus couldn't be a giant spider yet, but his hope was not lost. He decided to stay and enjoy the show.

26

THE SATANIC SINGULARITY, 2106

Ryan settled into a seat in the priest's office, which was disorganized in stark contrast to the sanctuary he'd just walked through. The desk was packed with papers, legal pads, and case folders, which Ryan shifted aside to make space for his phone. Setting it down, he began a new audio recording and looked around. He had never been in a Catholic church, but it was as expected. Polished pews. Stained glass. More formal than his typical interview settings, which tended to be more of the pubs, prisons, and front porches variety. The office was positioned at the back of the church and was bathed in dark brown wainscoting and lit with sconces. The shelves behind his desk were jammed full of books with the overflow spread on his desk. The priest's energy was rushed. He was apparently a busy man.

"Thank you for agreeing to this interview, Father McConnolly. You must have a packed schedule."

"Not a problem," said the old man with a serious face. "I think you are doing the world a favor by spreading the word about this issue."

"Well, thank you," Ryan said, wondering if the priest knew

how much of a skeptic Ryan still was, despite everything he'd been through with his own demon. Ryan saw himself as a good, objective reporter, and so approached any supernatural incidences case-by-case, erring on the side of disbelief. Not *everything* that startles someone at night is a demon. "Okay, let's start. There's been a rash of robot 'rebellion' and 'self-aware' robots in the past couple months. Why—in your opinion—is this happening? I want to hear it in your own words."

"Well, it's true roboticists have been unable to explain so far, but that's not because it's inexplicable," the priest said, knowingly. "It's because it is *not* a technical malfunction at all, nor are the robots intelligent. What is happening is demon possession. Coffee?" the Priest said and held up a stained carafe and paper cup.

"No, thanks," Ryan said, taking the pause to scribble notes about his surroundings—including the bottle of bourbon he spied next to the coffee maker. The priest poured himself coffee in a mug with dry brown drips on the outside.

"Okay," Ryan continued. "Even though a good portion of people don't believe in demons, we're at least used to the idea of humans being possessed by demons because it's a popular theme in horror films. Many are sort of open to the idea that it's possible for a demon to seize a human soul. But, without a soul, how is it possible for a robot to be possessed?".

"Ah, the key question," said Father McConnolly, nodding as he settled into his cracked leather desk chair. "A possessed robot looks very much like a possessed human. They carry on saying sacrilegious things, threatening violence, and so on. That's what we're seeing on the outside. However, from a technical standpoint, the possessed robot acts more like an inanimate object being controlled by a demon. Famously, you may have heard of demon-possessed dolls or perhaps mirrors. The robot, given that it is more object than human, is like a possessed doll, but much more powerful. Still, the recourse remains the same. Whether a person or an object is being possessed, demons must be cast out by rite of exorcism."

Father McConnolly's phone lit up on his desk just then. He politely ignored it.

"Has it worked?" Ryan asked, trying to picture Father McConnolly shouting during an exorcism like the priests in horror films.

"Yes," the priest said with a small smile. "I've personally cast out thirty-eight demons all over the Pacific Northwest. I've been getting calls from everywhere, though, because very few priests are taking this seriously and the Catholic church is painfully slow to update practices and policies. But people need help *now*," he said so emphatically Ryan believed in his sincerity. "I cannot in good conscience wait for the Vatican to give the thumbs up. More priests *need* to join me in this fight because I cannot do it all by myself."

"Why do you think they aren't taking it seriously?" Ryan asked hoping the priest would bad-mouth the Catholic church a little. The controversy would attract readers.

The priest heaved a long, slow sigh before responding. "Well," he said, "the videos out there of me performing exorcisms are unauthorized. I never asked for these videos to be taken, but people just do it. And then since these people who upload the videos don't have the reliable credibility a journalist does, it's too easy to cry *fake*." He paused and gave Ryan an imploring look that made him feel like the priest was depending on him to legitimize his exorcisms to the public. "The Vatican and the general public are skeptical of what I'm doing. You, though. You are an established journalist. People trust you and if you say it's real, maybe they will believe."

The phone lit up again. Ryan glanced at it. "You can take that if you need," he said.

Father McConnolly nodded, and picked up the phone, stepping away as he did so. Ryan examined the objects on the desk and wondered if they were exorcism tools. There was a wooden crucifix, a tiny glass bottle etched with another crucifix, rosary beads, and a long black stick with a forked metal tip.

"Do you want to see an exorcism?" the priest asked Ryan, startling him. He hadn't realized he'd come back into the office. Father McConnolly didn't wait for an answer, just began collecting supplies in a black medicine bag. He was going whether Ryan came or not.

"Definitely."

Ryan waited until they were settled into the Father's car before he resumed his questioning. The Father had to clear books and papers away from the front seat and add them to the mess of bags and fast food wrappers in the back.

"I have a question that might seem kind of silly," Ryan said, buckling his seatbelt. "Why not just turn the robot off? Or crush it or something? You could even control it remotely with a phone."

Father McConnolly gave him a sad smile. "Wouldn't it be nice if it were that easy? But I'm afraid turning the robot off doesn't work," he said. "Remember that a demon is supernatural, which means it will continue to move the bot regardless. It could even turn itself back on. If we crush the bot, the demon will likely leave the body of that particular bot, but will still linger and perhaps enter something or someone else in the immediate vicinity. No, in order for the demon to be truly vanquished, it must be cast back into Hell."

Ryan pictured a demon arriving back in Hell, a failure. How would the demon feel? Humiliated? Angry? Or would they just say *damn* and blow off some steam and have some drinks. Is hell really so bad?

"That doesn't sound like a punishment for the demon, though," Ryan said, curious. "Isn't Hell their home?"

"Yes, that's true. Home sweet home. But demons thrive on destruction and perversion. Up here on Earth is the only place they can feel fulfilled because there are good things here they can destroy. Hell is already a destroyed place. I imagine you like being home, but you wouldn't feel productive if you were there all the time, right?"

Ryan could see the logic. He nudged a stale French fry on the floor with his shoe, then looked in the back seat at the jumble of refuse, books, and tools.

"So why the cattle prod?" Ryan asked, pointing to the item in the backseat.

"It creates pain and weakens the demon. Robots may not feel anguish, but demons do," the priest said, not missing a beat.

"You must have done a lot of experimenting to figure that out."

"I did," Father McConnolly said with a grimace. "And I don't relish torturing anyone or anything. It's an unpleasant business. I once submerged a bot in water, but that created a dangerous situation in terms of being electrocuted."

Ryan waited quietly, hoping the priest would take that as an opportunity to monologue. He did not. Ryan's instincts told him he should tell the priest about his own demon experience, despite the fear that it would make him sound biased. After all, his instincts had made him successful.

Ryan cleared his throat. "I never speak about this publicly, but I've seen a demon." He paused, and snuck a glance at the priest, who merely nodded and kept his eyes on the road. "My Dad found this heavy metal record when he was a kid. It must have been at least fifty years old when he found it. Anyway, the record was somehow carrying a demon, which then moved to an old jack-in-the-box. My sister had the jack-in-the-box for a while and it was like her house was haunted—this was before we knew about the demon. Once she met him, she pawned it off on me, and then I met the demon too. Then I gave it to my dad," Ryan said, feeling a small wave of guilt. He wondered how much he should say, but then reasoned that unless the priest knew the whole truth, he couldn't offer any insight. "I felt bad about it, but I figured he was old enough that it wouldn't really matter. Then, one day my dad called me raving about his Patty, telling me that something was wrong with it, that it just up and left on him. It came back, but I wonder now if his Patty was possessed. The jack-in-the-box it was in had inexplicably been smashed to pieces, but I don't know the whole story—this is all pieced together based on bits the demon told me and bits my Dad told me."

"What is the name of the demon?" Father McConnolly asked quietly.

Ryan thought back to the day he gave the jack-in-the-box to his Dad. It had been six years ago. Ryan had mentioned the heavy metal record and his Dad had said a name.

"I don't know. My Dad may have said it, but I couldn't understand and then he seemed to forget. Bar-something. Funny thing is, though, the demon mentioned *your* name, now that I think of it. My partner told the demon we'd call a priest and the demon asked us if we knew Father McConnolly. Can demons know the future?"

Father McConnolly silently cocked his head in a way that said he didn't really know. Just then, they arrived. The priest drove towards a cluster of police cars and an ambulance in which a small family sat with blankets around their shoulders. Father McConnolly parked and an officer approached.

"Father. Glad you're here," the cop said gruffly. "This bot is kind of unpredictable right now. It attempted to hurt the family and then, when they escaped, it began destroying the house. Who's he?" he asked, jerking a thumb toward Ryan who was standing a few feet away taking pictures.

"This is Ryan Williams. He is a journalist. He'll be going in with me."

"It's not safe in there," the officer said.

"God will protect us," Father McConnolly said.

The officer couldn't argue with God.

The two approached the front door to the sound of crashes and clatters. A sulphurous smell poured out the front door. Inside, every shelf and table had been cleared of its contents. Anything that could have been broken was broken. Pottery and glass crunched underfoot.

"Father McConnolly!" a robot intoned and a multifunc rolled into the room.

Father McConnolly expertly flicked holy water and held up his crucifix while he began to speak in Latin. Ryan, frightened at the realization of the real danger he was in, dug the cattle prod out of the Father's bag instinctively and held it up in defense like a sword. When the robot charged them, he zapped it and the bot fell back. Rather than the growling and swearing Ryan had seen in exorcism movies, the robot emitted a cacophony of start up, shut down, alert, and reminder sounds.

Then the robot went silent. Dead.

"That was fast," Ryan said, incredulously, turning to the priest. Father McConnolly had not relaxed his stance yet, still mumbling under his breath with his eyes closed as if praying.

Out of nowhere, Nina strolled into the room in her rose scrubs, hair pulled back. "Ryan! It's me!" she called out.

"Aren't you my Dad's nurse?" Ryan asked, confused. What was Nina doing here in this random house? "Do you live here?"

"No. It's me, silly!" Nina said, her voice deepening. Ryan

watched as her features changed and morphed until Tom Cornetta III stood before him. Ryan lifted the cattle prod again.

"Geez, I thought we had a special connection. That night I had a whiskey with you and Beau," Tom Cornetta III—who Ryan realized in an instant was the demon from all those years ago—said before turning to Father McConnolly. "Did you know your friend here is gay?" he asked the priest. "How's the Catholic church feeling about that nowadays?"

"What is your name, demon?" Father McConnolly asked, his voice steady.

"How did you get out of the jack-in-the-box?" Ryan blurted out.

"Your old man let me out last year, and I've kind of been doing whatever I want since then. You ever watch Ultimate Robo Battle? I've been low-key possessing some fight bots. It's like I've found my calling!"

Father McConnolly splashed him in the face with holy water, which singed the demon's skin. Threads of smoke rose from his flesh.

"Enough!" the priest shouted.

The demon transformed once again. He became the clown. The springy, low-rent, wobbly clown. Ryan's fear was fresh. He had never seen the demon in this terrifying form. The priest read off passages in Latin once again, then asked for its name as the demon twisted in pain.

"Barbalus!" he moaned through ragged breath.

"Bulbous?" Ryan asked. It did sound vaguely familiar.

"No, you asshole, BAR-BUH-LUSS! Get it right!" the demon spat.

"Barbalus, by the power of Christ I command you to descend back to Hell!" Father McConnolly roared, and a box appeared at Barbalus's feet. *The* box. The wood box that had held him for so many decades. With a gust, Barbalus went downward, and it was like watching him spring out in reverse. The lid shut with an exclamation point of chiming notes from within the box, then dissolved into the floor.

Ryan could hardly believe everything he had just seen was real, but the air still smelled like that smell. It was like birthday candles just blown out. Plus boiled eggs.

"Is it over?" Ryan asked, his voice piercing the silence.

"This one is over." The priest was somber, serious.

"That was him," Ryan said. His grip on the cattle prod was so tight, it was difficult to loosen his hand enough to drop it. He felt shaky inside.

While the priest walked around the house praying blessings on every ravaged room, Ryan looked down at the multifunc on the floor. He thought that if he was in a movie, he might say something punchy like *Hope they paid for the extended warranty! But this was real life and it was fucking scary.*

He wondered if he should stay and help the family clean, but remembered he was still on assignment and needed to write while it was all still fresh in his head. He checked his phone to make sure it had been recording. It had. He dragged the timeline back to hear the last bit.

He heard everything as it was, except, oddly, Barbalus's voice was missing from the track. As if he and Father had been speaking to thin air. Then, a voice boomed so loud that he had to turn down the volume to keep the speaker from buzzing. It was loud enough to have tickled his hand with the vibrations.

"Ryan!" shouted Barbalus's voice through the phone. "Just wanted to throw a little something in here as a surprise. I really have been with your family a long time. We've had a few good memories. Anyway, you may remember me as Nina or you may remember me as Tom, but I *hope* you remember me as a scary fucking clown. See you in your dreams." Barbalus finished, sounding almost wistful at the end.

Ryan trembled. Would anyone believe this story? Would anyone believe this audio was genuine? Because if they didn't, it would destroy his credibility. Did he have a moral obligation to tell the story? Could he qualify it with disclaimers that left room for readers to doubt; nay, for himself to doubt, all that had occurred? It would be a cop-out. What kind of journalist did he want to be?

Father McConnolly and Ryan drove back to the church in silence. Ryan's heart was still jittery. The priest only seemed tired. Ryan's hand shook when he reached for the air conditioner button.

"You certainly gave me something to write about," Ryan said.

"I'm eager for the story to come out. You have the power to change things on a massive scale. It is a blessing. If people believe, there could be exorcists in every parish. Maybe even an emergency hotline to message." The priest chuckled at the idea.

In Hell, Barbalus found Grazul and knelt.

"Sir, I decided to come back to Hell for a bit-"

"As if you had a choice," Grazul interrupted.

Barbalus began again. "I *let* myself be driven back to Hell mainly because I wanted to give you a suggestion."

"What is it?" Grazul asked while distracting himself with a hangnail.

"I think we should stop the whole robot possession thing. I think it's better if the humans don't become so aware of us. We could just go back to doing subtle stuff."

"Oh man," Grazul said, chuckling. "I forgot we were even doing that! How's it been going?"

"We tore it up," Barbalus said, proud. "But they seem to be getting wise to us. There's this journalist who's going to write about it. Be pretty funny if his story comes out and then suddenly becomes totally irrelevant. Probably ruin his career!"

"Ok, yeah. Let's stop then." Grazul said disinterestedly. He beckoned behind him, and a dirty, cross-eyed man in chains and a torn purple robe crawled up into Barbalus's view.

"Hey, Dick. Chew this hangnail off for me, but *don't* open up a sore spot. Just the dry skin part." Grazul held his left hand down and Dick Williams gripped the hangnail between his yellowed teeth. His breath was raspy and lips dry and cracked. Barbalus watched as another man in a purple robe shambled up behind Dick and attempted to smooth out Dick's robe, but Dick simply kicked the man away while chewing at Grazul's finger.

"So... do I need you to sign something or..." Barbalus said, eager to finalize his plans.

"Oh, right," Grazul said, clearly bored. "I hereby declare that our possession of robots is over for the time being and all demons involved can go back to being subtle or whatever. Old school rules." With that, a burst of fiery red light rushed in all directions away from Grazul's body. "We cool?" he asked.

"Yeah. One more thing," Barbalus said, looking down at his feet. "I'd love if I could get together with you sometime and just pick your brain. I really want to get into the creative field."

"Ooh, okay," Grazul said. "My schedule's pretty busy, but I'm sure we'll work it out sometime. Call my assistant."

"I will," Barbalus said.

But he knew he had just been kicked down the road.

Grazul checked his hangnail and seemed to approve. He walked away and Dick followed on his knees with his chains rattling. Out of the darkness came a dozen sallow men in ragged robes, some with whitened eyes, following their master.

Barbalus was jealous. He wanted a crew of the dead to boss around. He wanted to be worshiped.

One day.

May as well relax in Hell for a while, Barbalus thought.

As if he had a choice.

27

BILLY'S REVIVAL, 2030

Billy unfolded an old card table in his garage, perfectly square with the vinyl surface peeling at one corner. He covered it with a long, rectangular table cloth that pooled on the floor. He frowned, and pushed the edges of the cloth under the table. At the center of the table, he placed a red satin pillow, and on the pillow, he placed his grandfather's dagger.

"God, I haven't seen that dagger in, what? Twenty-five years perhaps?" Tim mused. "Memories are just flooding back."

Tim's hair was graying now. So was Billy's.

Tim looked at the lawn chairs scattered in the filthy garage facing the makeshift altar, then down at his luxury suit. Billy envied the suit, but believed wholeheartedly that he would be wearing a suit like that in no time. Surely Grazul would honor the blood of his grandfather.

"Good thing I kept the robe all these years," Tim said, unzipping a garment bag and removing a freshly dry-cleaned purple robe.

"I found my grandfather's robe too," Billy said. He took the robe from an old cardboard box printed with the word "Crantran" and shook it out. "After I found out about the cult, I went looking around in my parent's attic and I found all this stuff. It must look just like your original meetings in the '90s!" he said, grinning.

"Not exactly," Tim said. "We had a dungeon to meet in. It had a pretty nice wet bar. Dramatic lighting. The whole nine yards."

"Well," Billy said, only slightly disappointed, "after we summon Grazul, I'm sure I'll be able to buy a nicer place soon. My memoirs are out of print, so..." he trailed off.

Billy put the purple robe on over his t-shirt and jeans. The hem dragged on the floor.

Greg and Pete entered the garage looking just as well-off as Tim with their glossy, gelled hair and their fancy cologne. *Sentience Pour Homme.*

"God, what are we doing here?" Greg mumbled.

A pair of Billy's friends, Jet and Manny, entered the garage behind them.

"Alright, let's get this cult started! Whoo!" Billy called out.

"Yeah! Let's do this!" Jet and Manny called back.

Greg and Pete searched for a place to hang their garment bags, but couldn't find one. They laid their bags across lawn chairs, grimacing slightly, and draped themselves in their robes. Jet and Manny set shopping bags on the floor and pulled out two purple hooded sweatshirts, which Billy had told them would probably be good enough for now. They pulled them over their heads, tags still dangling from the sleeves. The five followers sat in lawn chairs before Billy.

"Thanks for coming, everyone," Billy said, unsure of what they were supposed to do now. "As we can see, Tim, Greg, and Pete were in the original cult that my Grandfather led and, obviously, Grazul blessed them with wealth and power. What are you, a CEO, Tim?"

"I also have a side gig as a congressman," Tim said.

"Fantastic! I figured Grazul *must* be in my blood since my Granddad was so tight with him, so here we are! I'm the new Leader!"

Tim raised his hand. "Quick question," he said. "When and how did you manifest Grazul?" Tim crossed his arms in front of his chest.

"Good question," Billy said, hoping the men would buy into his unwavering belief in himself. "Well, I always kind of suspected my mother was some kind of satanist or witch or something. She took after her father. So it's in my family, right? Now, have I *talked* to Grazul? Have I been *possessed* by him? Who's to say?"

"I have a question too," Greg said. "I think I've established myself as anti-human sacrifice."

"I can vouch for that," Pete said.

"Thank you, Pete. Well, I'd like to continue to not participate in any killing. Can you speak to that?"

"Sure," Billy said. "The good news is, I agree. I skimmed over our sacred text and saw something about drinking blood, but I never dreamed we'd kill someone for it. My grandpa might have been a demon worshipper, but he wasn't a bad guy. I assumed you guys were never *murderers*. So," Billy said, pausing for dramatic effect. Pete and Tim and Greg seemed nonplussed, but at least Jet and Manny were into it. "*So,* what I did was I went on the dark web and bought some blood."

Billy retrieved a cooler from under the table. He struggled to open the lid and had to use the ornate dagger to pry it open. The fog of dry ice arose and spilled over the edges. Triumphantly, Billy lifted a ziplock baggy of thick, brownish liquid.

"There's no way I'm drinking that," Pete said, his mouth twisted in disgust.

"Don't worry," Billy said. "It came with this paperwork that says it's clean."

He held up a receipt. *Clean blood - $500.*

Jet raised his hand. "I have a question too. Do you have any whiskey? If you don't, I think Manny and I are going to make a liquor store run."

"There's beer in the fridge," Billy said, getting slightly annoyed.

"What kind?"

"Old Mountain Light with Lime."

"Yeah, we're gonna head out. We'll be back in a few."

Billy's two friends left the garage.

Billy sulked.

"Maybe you don't need a cult," Tim said. "Maybe you just need a job. I could probably find something for you. Do you have any special skills?"

"Would you guys just give this a shot with me? For your Leader? *Please*?" Billy asked.

Tim, Greg, and Pete looked at each other. They exchanged something silently with their eyes and then all shrugged.

"OK," Greg said, "For Dick. Our departed Leader. And for Grazul who blessed us richly."

Billy pumped a fist in the air with excitement. He poured the blood from the bag into a chalice, lit a candle, and turned down the lights.

"Oh Dark Lord Grazul! We summon you! We will drink the blood of... whoever. And we shall have riches and power and relationships with our siblings! I am your servant! Hear us Grazul! Hail the Dark Lord!"

"Hail the Dark Lord," the followers said, but Billy could tell their hearts weren't in it.

Billy stretched out his arms like a Messiah and lifted his head. The candle extinguished itself. In the darkness, two red glowing dots replaced Billy's blue eyes. The two red dots raised higher in the air as Billy's feet lifted off the ground. Billy hadn't known what to expect, but never dreamed he'd defy physics. His feeling of rapture was all consuming and he became unaware of anything else.

"Grazul!" Tim called out, "He's here! He's actually here!"

Tim, Greg, and Pete fell to their knees.

A voice came from Billy's mouth, but it wasn't his own.

"The grandson of your Leader is weak. Like his grandparents and parents, I call him The Disappointment. You shall not follow The Disappointment!"

The eyes lowered back down and faded. The room went silent and completely dark.

Billy fumbled with a lighter and relit the candle.

"Did it happen? I blacked out there for a second. Am I possessed by Grazul?!"

"I'm afraid not," Tim said. "That wasn't what it was like with Dick. Dick and Grazul would become one unified being at times. I'm sorry to say, Grazul basically disowned you. But try not to take it too hard. Like I said, maybe you just need a job. We can't all be cult leaders."

"Well, here! I'll drink the blood then!" Billy shouted, desperate to be their new Leader.

"Don't!" Greg said, but Billy had already begun drinking. He tipped the glass and drank all of the blood as if he had been stranded in a desert dying of thirst. In the dim light he appeared to have chocolate syrup around his mouth.

Pete found the light switch and turned it on.

Billy stood, green-cheeked and drowning in a baggy robe, dirty blood dripping down his chin. He fell to his knees.

"I don't feel so good," he said. On all fours, he felt ready to heave, but instead of vomiting he emitted a growl. He hyperventilated. Every exhale was like gravel rolling in his chest.

"Should we call 911?" Pete asked.

Billy looked up at him. His eyes went cloudy. Vacant. Billy

groped his way towards Pete baring his teeth and curling his fingers into claws.

"What are you doing?!" Pete shouted.

And then Billy was upon him, biting his neck. Ripping flesh away from Pete's still-living body.

Tim jumped at Billy and wrestled him to the ground. He pinned Billy's shoulders against an oil stain on the cement.

"Find something to stop the bleeding!" Tim shouted.

Greg found a bucket of absorbent shammies, grabbed a handful, and rushed to press the wad against Pete's neck. Pete's breathing slowed. He looked up at Greg. His eyes went white. He growled like a dog just before he bit into Greg's wrist.

Greg screamed. Blood sprayed. The white tablecloth was spattered with red.

Tim's body weakened in fear and panic. Billy took on unnatural strength as he sprang at Tim.

The garage door opened.

"Ok, we got some Crown Royal and then just some Canadian Club if you want to mix it with ginger ale," Jet said before he stopped short. Eight white eyes looked back at Jet and Manny. Without hesitation, the pair bolted back to their pickup truck, but Billy ran and leapt into the truck bed.

"Where do we go?" Jet shouted.

"The hospital?" Manny ventured.

Jet sped towards the hospital driving through red lights along the way. Billy's body wrapped its fingers tight over the edge of the truck and, hand over hand, reached for the window to the cab.

"Close it!" Jet said.

Manny pushed against the stubborn window.

"It won't shut!" he shouted, panicked.

When Jet slowed to take a turn, Billy tumbled towards the

window, bit Manny's finger and wouldn't let go. Manny pulled until his flesh tore away from the bone.

He screamed in agony.

When Jet stepped on the break at the emergency room entrance, all of their bodies rocked forward hard.

"I don't feel so good," Manny said.

His face was turning green.

An orderly approached the car with a wheelchair.

"That looks ouchie!" he said, looking at Manny's finger.

Billy leapt from the truck bed and Jet took the opportunity to run.

The orderly was not so lucky.

The Bite Virus outbreak began.

28

DRINKER OF STRANGE BLOOD: ON THE HERO WILLIAM "BILLY" BONFILS

I think William "Billy" Bonfils should be nominated for a posthumous Nobel Peace Prize. For the sake of disclosure, I should mention that Billy was my grandfather's cousin. He was dead long before I was born, but through his published memoirs and biographies, I've been able to learn about his life and he has become an admired figure in our family.

Billy endured a painful childhood with an abusive workaholic father, a disturbed mother, and two often dismissive siblings. (His siblings names were Gary and Gwyneth, but history knows them as Grady and Guadalupe and I shall refer to them as such.)

Billy's father Herbert "Bert" Bonfils was a successful businessman. Unfortunately, his business was multi-level marketing. At the time, it was legal to sell a huge stock of products to a gullible person eager to make quick cash, offer them no training or salary, and convince them they could sell the product in their spare time. What's more, they could earn more money by luring friends and family members into the same scheme. And it worked—at first. Eventually, though, the market became saturated with salesmen and no one to sell to.

When Billy wised up to this scheme, he bravely demanded that his father end this practice, to which his father replied, *"Son, if I wanted your opinion about whether or not I should fuck people over, I probably wouldn't be the kind of person that fucks people over."* After this, Billy began a letter writing campaign to politicians to build awareness of these business practices. (No copies or evidence of these letters exist, but why would his publisher have printed his memoir if they didn't research it themselves?)

Billy's mother, Missy Williams-Bonfils, engaged in dark spirituality. Rather than a warm motherly presence, Missy exuded an unsettling aura. Though she put on quite the act. There were the requisite hugs, kisses, hot dinners, field trip chaperoning, cheering at basketball games, and heart-to-heart conversations over cinnamon tea, but they all felt slightly "off" in Billy's mind. Was it to cover for something sinister? *Her* father was, after all, a documented cultist. This fact would lead to his undoing.

Billy's brother Grady, the oldest of the three Bonfils children, had a tendency to make poor decisions and required grace and bail-outs from Billy time after time. Grady then built undeserved wealth by joining his father's business. He invented a pseudoscientific device that was purported to alert users to the presence of androids. In hindsight we know it didn't work, but he profited from paranoia.

Guadalupe, the taciturn artist, was depressed, and often came to Billy with her broken relationships and turmoil as well. Guadalupe is still a celebrated poet to this day. She may not have been able to produce such wonderful work without Billy's encouragement.

Billy was the youngest, but had no one to look up to.

To his surprise and great pain, he was left out of his Grandmother's will, bequeathed only a sickly cat as a cruel joke.

He triumphed over this rejection by writing successful memoirs and, instead of being bitter, he cared for the cat until its peaceful passing in the sunny catnip garden he grew for it.

Billy was then bankrupted by the lawsuits thrust upon him by his family. They claimed his memoirs were inaccurate character assassinations.

Billy was a bold risk taker and decided to take his fate into his own hands by re-forming his grandfather's Cult of Grazul and drinking blood bought on the black market. He was in search of meaning and power. This decision was the result of his being abused. Can we really blame him for these choices?

Evidence has shown that Billy was Patient Zero in the Bite Virus outbreak.

Evidence, as well as time, has also shown that the Bite Virus saved humanity from climate change because of the drastic decrease in world population.

Trailblazers like these deserve to be honored so that they can continue to inspire young people like me. Because he was bold and brave enough to drink strange blood, I have lived.

29

BILLY FINALLY GETS HIS LIFE TOGETHER, 2029

"Well, Billy," Dr. Suarez mused, giving Billy the serene and patient look that all therapists must have to master, "the childhood you've described stands in contrast to the life you described in your memoir."

"Memoirs," Billy jumped in. "*Memoirs* as in plural. I wrote two. The second one wasn't such a hit."

"Pardon me, memoirs, although I should mention I only read the first one," Dr. Suarez admitted.

"So did everyone else."

Billy scratched at a blemish on the arm of the couch. Was it leather or vinyl? The stuffing appeared as a pinprick of white fluff.

"Well, back to what I was getting at," Dr. Suarez said, drawing his attention back. "In your book, you described a childhood where you were a hero rising above very serious family discord and abuse. In real life, however, it sounds like you had a distant father, a loving mother who may have drank too much, and average sibling rivalries. And who was it that started calling you The Disappointment?"

"Grandma. My parents said that she was starting to get

dementia or something, but looking back, she still drove a car and golfed and played bridge. I think she really just viewed me as a dud."

"Could you stop picking at the arm of the couch?"

Billy withdrew his hand and hugged a throw pillow instead.

"My sister was this burgeoning artist and my brother was athletic and so smart he skipped a grade. There was nothing really special about me. Still isn't."

"This may sound harsh, but—"

"Please!" Billy interrupted. "Be harsh. I need brutal honesty."

"It sounds like from a young age your family has had low expectations for you and you continued to plummet to their low expectations. Even though you aren't in touch with them very much anymore, you've continued as an adult to have difficulty maintaining a job, making wise decisions with money, or having relationships that aren't entirely self-centered. It's like you're fulfilling their prophesies."

"Ouch. Wow. When you put it like that, I sound like a real loser."

"Do you really think of yourself as a loser?" Dr. Suarez asked.

"Not until a few months ago. I started having trouble paying bills. I can't afford to date. It was kind of a wake-up call," Billy said quietly.

"What would a winner do?"

Billy began picking at the floral embroidery on the throw pillow.

"Transform. Physically, mentally, emotionally. Suck the blood of life."

"Marrow," Dr. Suarez corrected.

"Pardon me?"

"Suck the marrow of life. Thoreau."

"Whatever. I want something massive and impactful to take

hold of me and just sweep through the world. I want to leave a legacy!"

"There's no force that will swoop in and fix your life. You have to do that yourself. How are you going to do it?"

"I'm thinking of starting a career in direct sales."

Dr. Suarez bit her lip. "What else?" she said.

"Well, I want to be a better son," Billy ventured, glancing at Dr. Suarez, who nodded encouragingly. "My parents are moving out of my childhood home next month. I think I want to go help them clear out the house. Gwyneth and Gare Bear are going to gather their old stuff. I heard about it from Gare. Gwyn and Gare's bedrooms are still there just the way they left them. My stuff ended up in the attic and my mom turned my old room into an office."

"These are good starts. A job. Some selfless action. Good. It looks like our time is up for today."

"Gosh, I talked about all this stuff and completely forgot about the main reason I'm here," Billy said. He sat up and leaned in. "I'm looking for an angel investor for my new business. You were so highly recommended, I figured you must have money. You believe in me, right, Dr. Suarez?"

"Billy, if you want to transform your life, I believe you can do it."

"I'll take that as a Yes."

"But I don't get involved with patients' personal lives. Certainly not financially."

"I'll stop coming back then. I'm not your patient anymore. Now, I'm just a guy in your office here to tell you about a product that sells itself."

"No. I recommend you come back for further therapy."

Billy's face fell. He pushed himself up off the couch and felt a wave of cold now that he didn't have a pillow pressed against his body and a cozy couch under his keister.

"Billy," the doctor said. "Don't let it get you down. Keep trying."

"I will. You know what doctor? I will. And I really am going to make an impact on the world."

Billy reached for the door. He believed in himself to the point of madness.

"Billy," Dr. Suarez said.

Billy paused and looked back at her.

"You may want to consider something other than direct sales. Those companies are really predatory sometimes."

Billy nodded and resumed his confident stride. He felt like he could win a Nobel if he wanted to. Now that he had a little encouragement, nothing could stop him. Not economic hardship. Not rejection from a woman. Not climate change. Not the androids.

Nothing.

THE WILLIAMS FAMILY

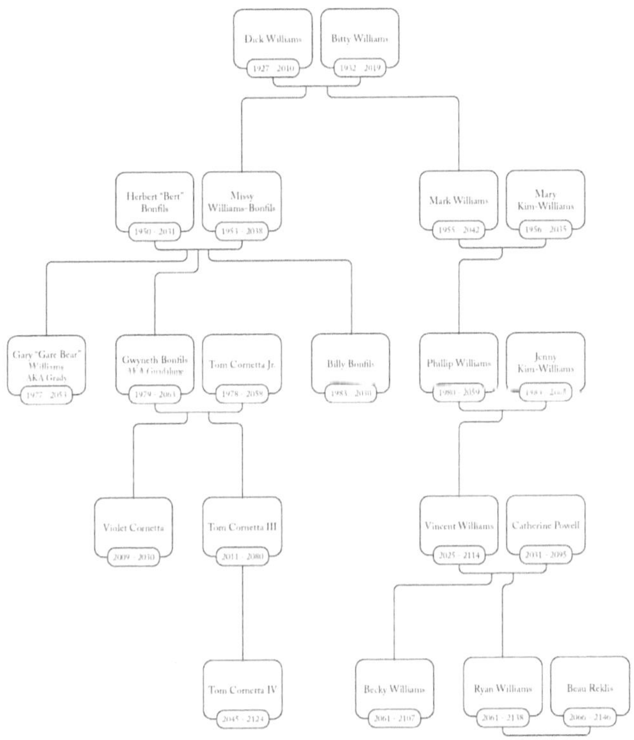

A BRIEF TIMELINE

40,000BC - 7000BC Modern men develop, but they aren't *special* like *us*.

7000BC - 5000BC The birth of God's mankind. That's you!

14 Unknown demon writes song that has satanic content when you play it backwards on the lute.

1981 The demon Barbalus is assigned to curse a heavy metal record sold to a teenage boy.

1991 Bitty Williams paints portrait of Jesus making eye contact with you, the viewer.

1992 Phillip Williams buys Barbalus' cursed heavy metal record secondhand.

1996 Grazul is conjured by Dick Williams.

2005 Bigfoot spotted by human for first time in thirty-four years.

2012 Portal technology developed, but is only a passing fad.

2020 Somebot releases their first "multifunc", a multifunctional robot personal assistant.

2021 The android detection/urinary tract infection prevention product *Crantran* is released.

2025 Diego Vidal's *Luminaria* multifunc is released.

2028 Human : Bot ratio work laws are passed and dubbed The Leisure Act.

2030 Somebot releases the Model30, an eerily humanlike multifunc. Its appearance gives everyone heebie jeebies.

2030 Bite Virus, a human population bottleneck event, occurs. 3.2 Billion people die worldwide.

2038 The demon Barbalus leaves his heavy metal record and enters an antique jack-in-the-box.

2040 No more Climate Change!

2106 The Satanic Singularity occurs.

2130 Billy Bonfils receives posthumous Nobel Prize.

2140 Climate Change!

2142 Tom Cornetta I unfrozen from cryogenic sleep to cheer everyone up.

Unknown future date Christ returns, looks nothing like Bitty Williams' portrait.

BIOGRAPHIES OF SOME CHARACTERS

Dick Williams, 1927 - 2010

Vessel for Grazul, secret(ish) cult leader, rich business guy. Dies at age 83 of natural causes. Goes to Hell. Thought he would be powerful in Hell. Grazul instead changes Dick's likeness to resemble Bitty's cross-eyed portrait of him and puts him in charge of manicuring his hooves and horns.

Bitty Williams, 1932 - 2019

Painter of awkward portrait of Christ, temporary owner of Mittens the cat. Dies at age 87 of natural causes. Goes to Heaven. Though Dick converted to Catholicism for her when they married in 1950, she discovers that the conversion was only feigned, but she kind of already knew that. God forgives her for treating Billy like a loser.

Missy Williams-Bonfils, 1953 - 2038

Book lover, alcoholic, heiress, definitely not a witch.

Herbert "Bert" Bonfils, 1950 - 2031

CEO of Crantran, workaholic.

Gary "Gare Bear" Bonfils; AKA "Grady", 1977 - 2053

Inventor of Crantran, android conspiracy theorist.

Gwyneth Bonfils AKA Gwyneth Bonfils-Cornetta, AKA "Guadalupe", 1979 - 2063

Notable poet. Dies at age 84 by drowning in the ocean. She knew she wasn't fit enough to go swimming, but, as a poet, couldn't resist. Her final poem was left on the beach and described sand as "fine descendants of Abraham."

Billy Bonfils - 1983-2030

Writer, good Samaritan sometimes, possibly guilty of cat manslaughter, Bite Virus patient zero, dies at 47 trying to create his legacy, wins a posthumous Nobel for accidentally stopping climate change.

Mark Williams, 1955 - 2042

Military man, recipient of Bitty Williams' Jesus portrait, buyer of cabin, first owner of jack-in-the-box that would later become cursed.

Phillip Williams, 1980 - 2059

Heavy metal fan, poor planner of family reunions, extremely hairy.

Vincent Williams 2025 - 2114

Only child, recipient of Bitty William's Jesus portrait, finder of vintage demon-possessed heavy metal album.

Becky Williams 2061 - 2107

Unofficial nominator of Billy Bonfils for a Nobel Prize, temporary owner of cursed jack-in-the-box, killed at 46 by a self-driving car that swerved to avoid hitting her more successful twin brother, Ryan.

Ryan Williams, 2061 - 2138

Writer of bestselling biography of Billy Bonfils *Drinker of Strange Blood*, broke the story of the satanic singularity with Father McConnolly which only temporarily damaged his otherwise illustrious career. Dies at age 77 while reporting on political unrest in the US by being hit in the head by a tear gas canister.

Father McConnolly, 2052 - 2115

Badass exorcist.

Stephen - 1997-2055

Dies at 58 by hitting himself in the back of the head with his own golf club. No one from work makes it to his memorial just like they didn't make it to his cookout last summer. Jerks.

Tom Cornetta I, 1955 - (cryogenically frozen in 2023)

Charming tv host beloved by all.

Tom Cornetta II, 1978 - 2058

Charming actor who cheated on wife Gwyneth Bonfils with an actress, but everyone still liked him because he was just so darn cute.

Tom Cornetta III, 2011 - 2080

Charming tv host, son of Gwyneth Bonfils.

Tom Cornetta IV, 2045 - 2124

TV host, but kind of disappointing in the charm department. Bares no offspring.

Tom Cornetta I, 2142

Unfrozen as a 68 year old man, hosts a revival of Silly Vids for one year, suddenly and rapidly ages 100 years on live television and crumbles to a pile of dust.

Diego Vidal - Birth and death date unknown

Peruvian-American roboticist, inventor of the luxury multifunc Luminaria, sexy genius.

OTHER TRIVIA

2030 Bite Virus Victims - Billy, Tim, Pete, Greg, Manny, Elise, Rodellee, Quince, Violet

Bite Virus Hero - Jenny Kim-Williams, wife of Philip Williams, Mother of Vincent Williams, at age 47 killed an estimated 35 Bite Virus Victims with a knife taped to a broomstick to save her family. Her victims included Rodellee, Elise, and Quince. She didn't know Quince personally, but could tell she was tacky.

The Satanic Singularity - The demon possessed robots killed an estimated 500,000 people worldwide. Though few believed demons were actually to blame, it was still commonly referred to as The Satanic Singularity. Ryan reported that the robots were demon-possessed, but his rather unscientific view was unpopular and temporarily marred his career. It was more commonly accepted that the singularity was a proper singularity and that when it appeared to be over, the robots were only pretending not to be self-aware. People continued to own robots out of convenience. Most believe they will attempt to take over again at unknown future date.

Somebot - The first company to produce multifuncs.

Luminaria - Not the first company to produce multifuncs, but the best.
182

Crantran - A subdermal implant sold and implanted by stay-at-home mothers that alerts users to the presence of androids[1] and prevents urinary tract infections[2] by releasing a constant stream of cranberry extract. Crantran fell out of favor during the Bite Virus outbreak because androids suddenly didn't seem like such a big problem.

---

1. Doesn't actually work
2. Actually does work

ABOUT THE AUTHOR

Kristin Hooker is a writer in Portland, OR.

9 781736 442616